"In the mean [could stay a]

"Stay at your place?" Charlotte echoed, knowing she should be pleased, but was momentarily horrified, and sounded it.

"Rather than book you into a hotel, I thought you could stay. Unless, of course, you have any serious objections to living under my roof for a short time?"

"W-well...no."

"I thought the press might have managed to convince you that no woman is safe when I'm around."

She didn't need convincing, Charlotte thought bitterly; she already knew that he was a ruthless womanizer.

LEE WILKINSON lives with her husband in a three-hundred-year-old stone cottage in an English village, which most winters gets cut off by snow. They both enjoy traveling and recently joined forces with their daughter and son-in-law to spend a year going around the world "on a shoestring," while their son looked after Kelly, their much loved German shepherd. Her hobbies are reading, gardening and holding impromptu barbecues for her long-suffering family and friends.

THE TYCOON'S
TROPHY MISTRESS

LEE WILKINSON

AT THE BOSS'S BIDDING

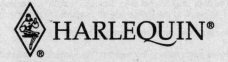

TORONTO • NEW YORK • LONDON
AMSTERDAM • PARIS • SYDNEY • HAMBURG
STOCKHOLM • ATHENS • TOKYO • MILAN • MADRID
PRAGUE • WARSAW • BUDAPEST • AUCKLAND

ISBN 0-373-82018-6

THE TYCOON'S TROPHY MISTRESS

First North American Publication 2004.

This edition published by arrangement with Harlequin Books S.A.

® and TM are trademarks of the publisher. Trademarks indicated with ® are registered in the United States Patent and Trademark Office, the Canadian Trade Marks Office and in other countries.

www.eHarlequin.com

Printed in U.S.A.

CHAPTER ONE

IN THE London headquarters of Wolfe International the man with the cool grey eyes paced the luxurious private office kept solely for his use, restless as a tiger in a cage.

What would he do if she didn't show, if she'd changed her mind?

Above the muted but ever-present background roar of Piccadilly's traffic he heard the high-pitched whine of the lift.

A moment later, pausing by the long narrow horizontal window between the two offices, he saw the door of the outer office open.

Screened by the cream vertical-slatted blind, he watched her walk into the empty outer office and stand by Telford's large, imposing desk.

A natural redhead, he judged—long-legged, slender and graceful, with an oval face, a straight nose, high cheek-bones, a determined chin and a mouth like a young Sophia Loren's.

Her hair was taken up into a smooth coil which served to emphasize her pure bone-structure, and from his vantage point he could see that her eyes slanted up a little at the outer corners. Disappointingly, he couldn't make out their colour.

She was so exactly like his dream of a perfect woman that she could have been built to his specification.

Though this woman was far from being a plastic, mass-produced, empty-headed doll type.

A special something—the alignment of her features maybe—made hers a fascinating face rather than merely beautiful. And, judging by the job she did and what he had already found out about her, she had brains and character.

Assets most of the others had lacked.

But until now, avoiding any risk of involvement or emotional blood-letting, he hadn't been looking for brains or character, merely a beautiful companion to decorate his arm at public functions and a beautiful body to take to bed at night. In short, his physical needs satisfied while his emotions remained placid, undisturbed.

This time, however, his emotions were anything but placid and undisturbed. He had wanted her fiercely, passionately, since the first moment he had set eyes on her some three months previously.

Then he had caught sight of her briefly just as he was about to leave for the airport and, knocked for six, had asked his Managing Director who she was.

'That's Tim Hunt's sister.'

The answer had shaken Daniel Wolfe badly and it was a moment before he said evenly, 'I wasn't aware he had a sister.'

'So far as I know it isn't common knowledge.'

'Personnel had no other Hunt listed.'

'Her name's Charlotte Michaels,' Telford told him as the two men took the lift down.

With a sudden stab of alarm Daniel demanded, 'Is she married?' He had always avoided married women like the plague.

'No, she's single.'

'Then why the different surnames?'

'I suppose, to be exact, I should have said she's Tim Hunt's *stepsister*.'

Daniel let his breath out slowly. 'That would certainly have made things clearer.' Then, thoughtfully, 'Have you any idea if she was close to her stepbrother?'

'I gather they were extremely close.'

'She wasn't at the funeral.'

'Charlotte was away when it happened. Not having had a holiday the previous year she'd taken five weeks off and, by the time she heard the news and flew home, it was all over.'

'How old is Miss Michaels?' Daniel pursued as they left the lift and made their way across the sumptuous marble-floored lobby to the main entrance where a limousine was waiting.

'I don't remember precisely. Twenty-five or six.'

'What exactly does she do?'

'Charlotte works with our main research team, analyzing current market trends and helping to predict future ones.'

'Been with the company long?'

'She started at the beginning of last year. Some time in February, I believe.'

'How about her private life? Any men friends? A live-in lover, for example?'

Telford's bushy eyebrows drew together in a frown. 'I really don't know.' It was obvious that the middle-aged MD disapproved of such a personal question.

'How does she get on with the men she works with?'

'Very well. Though she can appear a little aloof, she's always polite and friendly.'

'No office romance of any kind?' Daniel persisted.

'Not that I'm aware of. In fact, it's rumoured that since her engagement broke up earlier this year she's tended to avoid men.'

'I see. Is she good at her job?'

'Excellent. I'd say she has one of the best brains in the team. But as well as being clever she's genuinely nice and caring. She was extremely distressed by her stepbrother's death.'

Telford held open one of the heavy smoked-glass doors for his boss and, as though by way of warning, added,

'After reading the reports in the press, and hearing the office gossip, she became very upset and angry. She seemed to think that *you* were largely to blame for what had happened...'

Someone passed them, coming in, and the MD lowered his voice. 'She handed in her notice but I didn't want to lose her, so I told her to take some time off and think things over. I must admit I was both surprised and pleased when she chose to come back.'

Daniel's grey eyes narrowed.

Most of his previous women had been easy, almost boringly so. Discovering what he was up against told him that this one would be *anything* but easy. In fact, it might prove to be one of the biggest challenges he had ever taken on.

But it was typical of the man that he never for an instant thought of giving up. He had always been a man who knew precisely how to get what he wanted, and he wanted this woman. Wanted her more than he had wanted anything for a very long time.

And he intended to have her.

He wondered briefly whether to postpone his flight, go back and speak to her now, introduce himself.

If he could bring everything out into the open he would be able to start his campaign immediately, as he was itching to do, rather than wait.

But a sure instinct warned that if he made his move too soon he could spoil everything. It would pay to be patient, to allow more time to elapse. That way heated emotions would have a better chance to cool.

So, reining in his impatience, he handed the waiting chauffeur his small amount of luggage, shook hands with Telford and reluctantly climbed into the limousine to be driven through the sunny September streets to the airport.

Back in New York he had hired Alan Sheering, a discreet London investigator—based, ironically enough, in Baker

Street—to dig out everything he could about Charlotte Michaels and any possible boyfriend.

Sheering reported that, apart from her ex-fiancé, he could find no trace of any boyfriends past or present. He had also come up with a goodly amount of general information, including the fact that she had always enjoyed travelling and had expressed a wish to one day visit the States.

Using that as a starting point, Daniel had decided on a plan. A plan that would, if it worked, bring him a step nearer to his goal, by providing a change of scene and distancing both Charlotte Michaels and himself from what had happened in London.

Sounding brisk and businesslike, he had phoned Telford. 'I've decided that, in order to provide firsthand experience of how things are done both in the States and the UK, there should be some exchange of personnel.'

'What exactly do you have in mind?' his MD had asked cautiously.

'As a trial run, say, one of our London-based Research Team changes places with one from New York to study the possible differences in market trends.'

'For how long?'

'Six months. A year. We'll see how it goes.'

'Have you anyone particular in mind?'

'From this end an up and coming youngster named Matthew Curtis is eager to give it a try.'

'And from the London end?'

Bearing in mind that the move had to be *voluntary*, Daniel suggested as casually as possible, 'Suppose you see who's interested?'

If she didn't take the bait he would have to think of something else.

'I don't know how well such a scheme will be received,' Telford said slowly. 'You see, the majority of our team are either married or have partners, and as most of them also have young families they're hardly likely to welcome so much upheaval. Still, I can always circulate a memo and see what response we get.'

'Do that.' Daniel crossed his fingers and waited with what patience he could muster.

In the end, only two people put in for the temporary transfer—Paul Rowlands, the newest member of the team and, to both Telford's and Daniel's surprise, Charlotte Michaels.

Briefly, Daniel wondered what had made her apply. But, if Sheering was right, there was nothing to keep her in London and perhaps she felt she needed a change of scene, a chance to leave the past behind.

Delighted that things had worked out so well, he could hardly control his impatience. These last weeks had seemed endless, making him feel restless and dissatisfied. Eager as a boy.

'Are you thinking of interviewing the candidates yourself?' Telford had asked.

Wanting everything to seem routine and above board, Daniel had answered, 'No, I'll leave that to you. All the same, as it's my baby and I've a personal interest in the outcome, I'd like to hold a watching brief, so when you decide on the day I'll make a flying visit. But don't advertise it,' he added crisply, 'and don't send the car to the airport. I'd prefer to slip in unnoticed.'

If his MD wondered at these instructions he said nothing.

Now the big day had arrived, and things were going well so far. Telford had talked to Paul Rowlands that morning and been unimpressed, convinced that he was not yet ready to benefit from such a move.

Now, after lunch, it was Charlotte Michaels' turn.

Waiting impatiently for her to arrive at Telford's office, Daniel had half wondered if she really was as lovely as he'd first thought her. Suppose on second sight he was disappointed?

But when she finally appeared he sighed. She was even more beautiful than he remembered and, as if he had carried her picture in his mind, oddly familiar.

Though he still didn't know what kind of voice she had, what her smile was like, or what pleased her most when she was being made love to.

But it would be fun finding out, he told himself with anticipation.

As he watched her through the blind he noticed that she waited quietly for Telford, without fidgeting or showing obvious signs of impatience.

Yet a certain tension in the slim shoulders told him she was nowhere near as calm as she had first appeared. That the outcome of this interview *mattered* to her.

She glanced down and, with the first hint of nervousness she had betrayed, brushed an invisible speck from the lapel of her charcoal-grey jacket.

Just watching her hand lightly brush the curve of her breast brought a sudden rush of desire that surprised him with its strength and urgency. It sent his blood surging through his veins, clawed at his insides and urged him to walk out and chance his arm at once, rather than have to endure another endless period of waiting.

But at this point, as she had readily walked into the trap he had set with such care, it would be idiotic to risk losing the game. Though when she had officially been offered the transfer it might be possible to hurry things along a bit.

While Charlotte waited for Mr Telford she made an effort to calm her nerves and concentrate on the coming interview. If only she could get this transfer to the States...

After fruitlessly racking her brains for a way forward the

memo suggesting the exchange of personnel had come as a heaven-sent opportunity.

Of course she might be nowhere near Daniel Wolfe's office. She might not even be based in the same building. But, as he lived in New York, she had more chance of meeting him there than she did on one of his infrequent visits to the UK.

She knew when he visited Wolfe International's London headquarters by the stir his arrival inevitably caused amongst the rest of the staff, but she had never set eyes on him in person. All she had seen were pictures of him in glossy magazines or the society pages.

Tall and broad-shouldered, with dark hair that curled a little, a bony nose and light, piercing eyes set deep beneath well-marked brows, he was undeniably handsome.

Though not in the film star sense.

His was a lean face, tough and attractive, with a cleft chin and a mouth that had affected her strangely, always managing to send little shivers down her spine.

In the more sensational sections of the press he was often referred to as a latter-day Lothario, and frequent stories appeared about him and his latest 'conquest', some of which verged on the scurrilous.

Until a matter of months ago, repelled by such blatant sexuality, her instinct had been to avoid him at all costs.

Now things had altered completely. Meeting him, getting close to him, had become her only aim in life. Her mission.

On his last visit, despite all her efforts, she hadn't even managed to catch a glimpse of him. When she had finally thought of a reason to go up to the top floor executive suite it was to discover he had just that minute left for the airport.

Instead of making her give up her failure only served to stiffen her resolve.

During the following weeks, while trying to work out

some practicable strategy to achieve her goal, she had kept an eye on the papers and learnt all she could about him.

A top-flight Anglo-American entrepreneur from a wealthy background, he was known in the business world for his ability and in the outside world for his philanthropy.

A man who was said to work hard and play hard, Daniel Wolfe was today's hottest news, the centre of media attention on both sides of the Atlantic.

With an English mother and an American father, he had been educated at Columbia and Cambridge and, after graduating, had taken over the running of his godfather's ailing software company.

When that was firmly on its feet he had diversified, buying up other rocky companies and doing the same for them.

Now, at barely thirty, he was a multi-millionaire. Admired. Envied. Feared. Respected. Occasionally reviled.

In spite of so much coverage, he managed to keep his private life private. So, though Charlotte was soon familiar with his public image, she was able to glean little about the man himself.

In a recent article in *Top People* he'd been described, more temperately, as an unrepentant bachelor. But a bachelor who liked women. Especially beautiful women.

When, after each London visit, pictures of him appeared in the newspapers, there was always a willowy blonde or a redhead clinging to his arm.

Cursed with the kind of looks that attracted the opposite sex like a magnet, Charlotte had often wished she were plain. It would have saved a great deal of hassle, and made life so much simpler.

Entranced by her face and figure, men had been pursuing her since she was fifteen. Their unwanted, unlooked-for attentions, their sheer persistence, had driven her to hide behind a cool, impenetrable façade that only Peter had ever managed to breach.

And then it had been for all the wrong reasons.

Poor Peter.

But if her despised beauty could seriously attract Daniel Wolfe it would be worth all the problems it had caused in the past.

She had never imagined herself using her looks to try to ensnare a man, but knowing she was the type of woman he went for was an unexpected bonus and helped to bolster her determination.

But if he invariably went in for the kind of casual relationships where no feelings were involved the whole thing might well be impossible.

To succeed in what she was hoping to do, not only had she got to make him *want* her, somehow she had to make him fall in love with her...

As the office door opened and Mr Telford came in she looked up, a mite flustered, her cheeks growing hot as though he could read her thoughts.

Crossing to his desk, the tall, grey-haired MD said, 'Charlotte, my dear, do sit down. I'm sorry to have kept you waiting. I got held up at lunch.'

Taking a seat opposite, she strove to look cool and collected, as though the outcome of the interview didn't matter all that much.

His light blue eyes kind, Telford asked, 'So you're still interested in the move to New York?'

'Yes.' She hoped she didn't sound as breathless as she felt.

'Quite sure? It might mean having more contact with Mr Wolfe.' It was as far as he could go by way of warning.

'Absolutely.' She answered steadily.

It seemed that she had decided to put the past behind her. Relieved, he asked, 'Perhaps you'd like to tell me why?'

She had expected the question and rehearsed her reply.

'Apart from the fact that a firsthand knowledge of American market trends could prove to be invaluable, it would be a good chance to compare the way different teams work. I understand the New York team are usually extremely accurate with their predictions. I thought I might learn something.'

'A text-book answer,' he remarked with a smile. 'Though I rather suspected you had a more personal reason for wanting this move?'

She froze. It seemed he *knew*.

But he couldn't possibly know.

'How do you mean, a more personal reason?'

A twinkle in his eye, he said, 'Didn't you once tell me you'd like a chance to live in New York?'

'Yes. Yes, I did... I'm just surprised you remembered.' Then boldly, 'Does having a personal reason disqualify me?'

'Of course not. The mere fact that you *want* to live there is a big plus.'

Her sigh of relief was audible.

'In my opinion you're the candidate best suited to the move and, though I'm sure they'll miss you on the team, I'll put your name forward to Mr Wolfe.'

'That's marvellous.' She smiled at him brilliantly.

Blinking, he thanked the Lord that he was a very happily married man. Though she had been working for Wolfe International for almost two years, her beauty never failed to move him.

'If he's in agreement, which I'm sure he will be, all your travelling expenses will, of course, be met and you'll have the use of a company flat. Any idea how long it will take you to get organized for the transfer?'

'I can be ready as soon as you wish.'

The sooner the better.

'With Christmas less than two weeks away, I imagine

some time around mid-January should be fine. Will leaving your present accommodation give you any problems? I mean from a practical point of view?'

'No. I share a rented flat with an old school friend. Carla should have no trouble finding someone to take my place while I'm away.'

'Excellent… Then, as soon as I've had a word with Mr Wolfe, I'll let you know.'

'Thank you.' Her legs not quite steady, Charlotte made her way back to her own office—one of a row of small offices, little more than cubicles, that made up Research and Analysis—and sat down at her desk.

Her thoughts were chaotic, tumbling over each other like clowns in a circus ring. She had succeeded in taking the first step.

So long as Daniel Wolfe raised no objections…

But why should he? She and Tim had different surnames and, out of the country when it all happened, she hadn't been involved in any way, so he would have no idea there was any connection.

Charlotte felt her whole body tense as once again the hatred and anger rose up inside, sharp and biting, bitter as gall on her tongue.

After leaving college, and the somewhat wild bunch he had run around with, Tim had seemed to lose a lot of the feckless ways that had so worried her.

Settled in his new job with Wolfe International—a job Charlotte's recommendation had managed to get him—and confident about the future, he had fallen in love with Janice Jeffries, a pretty young blonde who had worked in the next office.

Janice, in her turn, had been fascinated by the young fair-haired giant with sparkling green eyes and a winning smile.

Discovering that the attraction was mutual, within a very short time they had arranged to move in together and had started to make plans to get married some time in September.

With Tim to support money had been very tight and Charlotte had taken no holidays since starting in her present job. She had five weeks due to her, so when Carla and she were offered a two-berth, last-minute cancellation on a 'roughing it' sailing trip around the Greek Islands she had gone off happily, not at all concerned about leaving the young couple.

While they were away it had happened, coming out of the blue swiftly, shockingly, and by the time the news had filtered through to them, and they had arrived back from Athens, it was too late.

Apparently trying to drown his sorrows, Tim had swallowed a lethal cocktail of drink and drugs.

He was dead and buried.

There was nothing anyone could do.

Though the verdict had been an unequivocal Accidental Death, the gutter press had somehow scented a story. Discovering that there had been a fight in one of the offices of Wolfe International between the dead man and Daniel Wolfe himself they were enjoying a field day.

Having managed to dig up the fact that Tim's fiancée had been involved, they were suggesting a love-triangle and hinting at possible suicide.

Blaming herself, Charlotte had bitterly regretted going away. If she had been at home things might have been different.

No, *would* have been different. If what the newspapers were suggesting was true, she would have been there for Tim, as she had been every day for the past five years…

The office door opening made her jump. She glanced up, her expression bleak.

'Don't look so anxious.' Mr Telford smiled at her. 'I've spoken to Mr Wolfe and he's quite willing to go along with my recommendation. There's only one thing; he'd like you to travel over to the States as soon as possible so you can get settled in before Christmas.'

Charlotte bit her lip to hold back the sudden surge of excitement.

Misreading her reaction, Mr Telford suggested, 'But perhaps that's too soon? I'm sure Mr Wolfe will understand if you'd prefer to be at home with your loved ones over Christmas?'

She shook her head. 'I've no loved ones left to be at home with. That's one of the reasons I applied for the move,' she added quietly.

Recalling not only the break-up of her engagement but what had happened to her stepbrother, and upset by his own unthinking blunder Mr Telford looked distressed. 'Please forgive me, my dear. I'm afraid I wasn't thinking.'

'That's all right.' Then, with a determined smile, 'Christmas in New York should be wonderful.'

'I hope it will be.'

'You're very kind,' she said warmly.

He harrumphed before asking, 'How do you stand as far as your work's concerned? Can some other member of the team take over?'

'That shouldn't be necessary. I can finish my latest report this afternoon.'

'So when do you think you can be ready to travel?'

Adrenalin pumping through her bloodstream, she told him, 'All I have to do is pack, so I could be ready to leave by tomorrow... If it's possible to get a flight at such short notice?'

'Our company have a big stake in one of the transatlantic airlines so that shouldn't prove to be a problem. I'll ask Mr Wolfe's secretary to make all the arrangements. She'll give you any other necessary information and organize a car to take you to the airport, where a ticket will be waiting for you. Needless to say, the company will be happy to defray any other travelling expenses you may incur, and this month's salary cheque will be paid into your bank as usual.'

'Thank you.'

Well aware that she had had to cope with more than enough heartbreak, at the door Mr Telford turned and said, 'You will take care, won't you...?'

Though it was, strictly speaking, none of his business, he was uneasy about Daniel Wolfe's barely concealed interest and his motive for what Telford was beginning to suspect had been a *contrived* move.

But, knowing how Charlotte felt about Wolfe, common sense told him that she was hardly likely to be in any danger.

Smiling, she answered, 'Of course.'

'And don't forget to come back to us.'

For an instant her smile faltered. She had already faced the fact that it would be impossible for her to return to Wolfe International. That chapter in her life was over.

Whether or not she succeeded in her mission, it would be time to put the past behind her, *if she could*, and move on...

But she *would* succeed, she vowed. She *had* to succeed to make the rest of her life worth living.

The bus, its grimy windows filmed with a fine drizzle, crawled through the heavier-than-usual Thursday evening traffic like a wounded snail.

By the time Charlotte got off at Belton Street and let herself into the Bayswater flat, her first, almost sick, excitement had seeped away.

So had her confidence.

As naturally tidy as her flatmate was untidy, she hung up her coat and suit jacket before going through to the bright little kitchen.

Carla, who looked like a cat, had all the subtlety of a Rottweiler and was fond of quoting platitudes. She was standing by the stove.

Her short black hair standing up in spikes, her triangular face a little flushed, she was stirring a pan of herby-smelling sauce with one hand and feeding long sticks of pasta into furiously bubbling water with the other.

Looking up, she said, 'I thought we'd have Spag Bol tonight, if that suits you?' Then, without waiting for an answer, 'What happened? Did you get it?'

'Yes, I got it.'

'Brill! So you're on course at last. How long will you be away?'

'I don't know. It all depends on how things go. The memo said six months, possibly a year... But I'm hoping to be home much sooner than that. I suppose you'll get someone else to share the rent?'

Carla who, with another friend, Macy, ran a small but very successful boutique, shook her head. 'I doubt it. It's not really necessary, and I don't know how I'd get on living with someone else.

'Any idea when you'll be going?'

'Tomorrow.'

'Tomorrow!' She sounded staggered. 'Why so soon?'

'They want me to get settled in before Christmas. You don't mind, do you?'

'Of course I don't mind. To tell you the truth, Andrew has been pressuring me to go up to Scotland with him on the 23rd. His family live in Dundee.'

'You didn't mention it.'

'I couldn't decide whether or not I wanted to go.'

Realizing that Carla had been unwilling to leave *her*, Charlotte could only feel grateful for such a loyal friend.

Knowing from past experience that her flatmate was uncomfortable with any undue display of sentiment, she merely said, 'But you'll go now, I hope?'

'I expect so. Though the shop's bound to be busy, Macy has offered to hold the fort for a couple of days in exchange for extra time off at New Year.'

Fishing out a strand of spaghetti and pinching it between her finger and thumb, Carla went on briskly, 'This is done, so I'll start dishing up. You can fill me in on all the details while we eat, and afterwards I'll help you with your packing.'

Then with satisfaction, 'It's a jolly good job I bullied you into buying all those new clothes in the autumn sale...

'Tell you what—' she continued, putting down two steaming bowls '—get some wineglasses out and we'll have a bottle of plonk to celebrate. When you've got your claws into Daniel Wolfe and brought him to his knees, we'll have champagne.'

'I don't think I can go through with it,' Charlotte admitted in a rush.

'Of course you can go through with it!' Carla's dark eyes flashed. 'That kind of swine ought to get his comeuppance.'

'But, even if I can attract his attention in the first place, I don't think I'm a good enough actress to pretend to like a man I loathe and detest.'

'Certainly you are. Didn't you play the *femme fatale* opposite that revolting Keith what's-his-name when the Sixth Form put on *Someone Like You*?'

'This isn't the same...'

'You can do it!'

'I'm not so sure... The thing is, as well as being an extremely wealthy man, Daniel Wolfe's got loads of sex-appeal, so he's—'

'How do you know he's got loads of sex-appeal?'

'I've seen pictures of him in the papers.'

'Newspaper pictures can give a false impression.'

'He's always got a woman clinging to his arm.'

'That could be something to do with his money. You know what they say about millionaires—some women will love them if they're bald and hideous and only four foot two.'

'He must be at least six foot and he has plenty of hair. Added to that, he's undeniably attractive.'

'Close to, I bet you he's wall-eyed and has halitosis,' Carla said sourly.

Charlotte smiled fleetingly. 'Just in case I *do* manage to get close to him, I rather hope not. But what I'm trying to say is, apart from being rich, he's clever and intelligent. I don't know if I can attract someone like that.'

Carla lifted her eyes to heaven as though praying for patience. 'You've been attracting the opposite sex since you were at school, without even trying.'

'But Daniel Wolfe is *different*. He lives in a different world and with no lack of women to choose from he may not fancy someone like me.'

'He'll be interested.'

'How can you be so sure?'

'He's a man, isn't he?'

'Yes.'

'And straight?'

'Almost certainly.'

'Then, mark my words, he'll be a pushover.'

CHAPTER TWO

HER brain stuck on a mental treadmill, thinking, planning, analyzing, unable to rest, Charlotte lay awake for most of the night. She got up the next morning heavy-eyed and headachy, and pulled on her old woollen dressing-gown.

Outside it was grey and gloomy, with lingering patches of mist. Her father would have referred to it as 'one of the dark days before Christmas'.

When she trailed through to the kitchen Carla, fully dressed and ready for her usual early start, was making toast and coffee.

'You look like something the cat dragged in,' she remarked bluntly.

'I *feel* like it,' Charlotte admitted.

'No beauty sleep?'

'Not much.'

'You'll have to do a lot better than that. If Daniel Wolfe could see you now, he'd run and hide.'

While they ate breakfast together she remarked thoughtfully, 'I reckon your best bet would be to appeal to his protective instincts, supposing he's got any. In my experience most macho men like the ''wide-eyed and helpless'' bit.'

'I'm not sure I can do wide-eyed and helpless,' Charlotte objected.

'Try. It feeds their egos, believe me.'

'I do believe you, but—'

'How far do you intend to go? To hook him, I mean. You don't plan to go to bed with him?'

A shiver running down her spine at the very thought, Charlotte said vehemently, 'No I most certainly don't!'

'Not that you couldn't use a spot of fun in your life...'

'That kind of excitement I can do without.'

'Well, if his reputation is anything to go by, he must be pretty good in bed and in your place I'd give it a whirl.'

'With a man like that?'

'As far as I'm concerned, life's a bowl of cherries. You have to spit out the stones and enjoy the flesh.'

'I don't seem able to,' Charlotte admitted. 'I often wonder if there's something wrong with me.'

'The only thing wrong with you is your pride. And pride builds a lonely house. But a word of caution... If you *do* mean to keep saying no, just watch yourself. Don't let the big bad Wolfe get you alone. From all accounts he's a born seducer and you never know, if he's used to getting his way, he may turn nasty...'

After issuing a spate of last-minute warnings and advice Carla gave her a quick hug. 'I'd better go. Fridays are always busy and so close to Christmas it's bound to be hectic.

'Oh, by the way, I've left your Christmas present on the bookcase. I haven't had time to wrap it, so you can use it as soon as you like.'

At the door she turned to say, 'Keep in touch. I'll miss you.'

When Charlotte went through to the living-room she found one of the boutique's elegant black and gold bags on the bookcase.

It contained three pairs of pure silk stockings and a bottle of Dawn Flight, her favourite perfume.

Smiling fondly at the other girl's absurd generosity, she went to fetch the Carillon Trilogy, which Carla had wanted.

Enquiries had proved it to be out of print, but after weeks of searching Charlotte had been lucky enough to find the set in a second-hand bookshop.

After she had showered, made-up with care and twisted her dark red-gold hair into a shining coil, she put on the sage-green suit and oatmeal blouse she had left ready and zipped up her case. Then, feeling tense and jumpy, she went to stand by the window of the basement flat.

She was looking up at the damp street when a sleek dark blue limousine with tinted windows stopped by the spiky wrought iron railings.

A moment later a uniformed chauffeur descended the steps and knocked at the yellow-painted door.

She hurried to open it.

Young and smart, he touched his peaked cap. 'Morning, Miss Michaels.'

'Good morning.'

'May I take your luggage?'

'Thank you.'

While he dealt with her case, Charlotte locked the door and put the key through the ornate letter-box, before following him up the area steps.

Having closed the boot he sprang to open the door of the limousine.

He couldn't have been more on the ball if he'd been chauffeuring Daniel Wolfe himself, she thought, secretly amused by his super-efficiency.

Head down, she had started to climb in before she realized that a man with dark hair, wearing a charcoal-grey business suit and a muted shirt and tie was already sitting there.

Surprise making her miss her footing, she stumbled and ended up almost in his lap, her face only inches from his, the warmth of his breath on her lips.

Steadying her until she was properly seated, he picked up the shoulder-bag she had dropped and handed it to her. 'I'm afraid I startled you.' He had an attractive voice.

'I just wasn't expecting…' As she realized who her fellow passenger was, the words tailed off.

No, it *couldn't* be.

But it *was*.

Although she had only seen pictures of him, there was no mistaking that tough, charismatic face and the arrogant tilt of that dark head.

In the flesh he was even more sexy than his pictures had led her to believe, and Carla had been quite wrong. His breath was fresh and sweet and the eyes that looked straight into hers were amazing—a brilliant silvery grey, their heavy lids fringed with dense, sooty lashes.

Her heart started to race and her breathing became shallow and impeded, while a quiver of pure hatred ran through her.

She was staring into those handsome eyes as though mesmerized when he reminded her politely, 'Don't forget to fasten your seat-belt, Miss Michaels.'

But her brain seemed to have slowed to a standstill and was unable to direct her fingers. When she had made a couple of fumbling, unsuccessful attempts, he leaned over and fastened it for her.

As the car slid smoothly away from the kerb, he felt a boyish urge to punch the air in triumph. After all these months of waiting, here she was at last, sitting beside him.

Close up, she was stunning. Her skin was flawless, a creamy gold, rather than pallid, as some natural redheads were. And those eyes! Daniel had been making bets with himself as to what colour her eyes would be. Probably blue, he'd decided. Blue he could happily live with, but that clear, dark green was absolutely breathtaking.

Not for the first time he found himself regretting what had happened. It could make getting anywhere with this gorgeous woman next door to impossible.

Though she was looking at him in a way that made him

strongly suspect she already knew who he was, he decided to take the plunge and bring things into the open. 'I guess I'd better introduce myself. I'm Daniel Wolfe.'

He held out his hand.

Like someone in a dream, Charlotte took it.

His palm was cool and dry, his handclasp firm, but she would sooner have touched a snake and she was already withdrawing her hand before he said politely, 'I'm pleased to meet you, Miss Michaels.'

Stunned by this surprise encounter, she made no reply. Her brain seemed jarred, incapable of coming to grips with the situation. All she could think was that *it was too soon. She wasn't ready.*

When she continued to sit as still and blank-faced as if she were having a passport photograph taken Daniel held his breath.

If she believed only a fraction of what the gutter press had printed she still had no reason to love him and, his usual confidence deserting him at times, he had wondered uneasily what her reaction would be when they finally came face to face.

Yet it was a hurdle he had to get over, and now the moment had arrived all he could do was wait for the recriminations.

But, apparently thrown by the unexpectedness of the meeting, she remained silent.

Letting his breath out slowly, he went on, 'As we were travelling at the same time I thought we might as well share a car to the airport...'

Charlotte, who had been struggling to gather her wits, blurted out the first thing that came into her head. 'I had no idea you were in London... That's why I was so surprised when you introduced yourself.'

Registering that she had a lovely voice, low and slightly

husky, he remarked, 'I got the impression that you knew who I was *before* I introduced myself?'

'Yes, I knew,' she admitted.

'But we've never actually met.'

'No,' she agreed.

'I presume you've seen me at the office?'

'No.'

'Out and about, socially?'

Shaking her head, she pointed out, 'We're hardly likely to move in the same social circles.'

'This beats I Spy.'

Momentarily failing to understand, she said, 'I beg your pardon?'

Straight faced, he explained, 'As a young child I used to get bored travelling in a car. My mother tried giving me books but looking down made me sick, so we always played I Spy With My Little Eye. I was just remarking that this particular guessing game beats it.'

Annoyed that he was making fun of her, she said crisply, 'I've seen pictures of you in the papers.'

But pictures hadn't had this impact. Pictures hadn't prepared her for the man himself.

He sighed. 'It was just getting exciting, and now you've gone and spoilt it.'

'Well, we can always play I Spy.'

As soon as the words were spoken she wished them unsaid. She was supposed to be trying to charm him, not trying to cut him down to size.

She couldn't afford to hurt his feelings. Like most men of his ilk he probably had a fragile ego and no sense of humour.

But a split second later he proved her wrong by bursting out laughing. He had a nice laugh, quiet and infectious, not the kind of hearty guffaw she so disliked.

A gleam in his eye, he said, 'I'm forced to admit that these days I prefer more grown up games.'

'I'm aware of that.' She had had tragic proof of his liking for 'grown up games', and all at once she wanted to fly at him, to rake her nails down his handsome face until she drew blood.

Regretting the teasing remark that had prompted such an icy response, Daniel sat quite still, watching her intently, braced for the worst.

But, already ashamed of that primitive urge to violence, and reminding herself that if she was to succeed in her campaign he mustn't know about her connection with Tim, Charlotte reined in her anger.

Making a great effort she added lightly, 'In every picture there's been a different woman on your arm, and the papers have frequently referred to you as a latter-day Lothario with a string of notches on your bedpost.'

'At times their stories have bordered on the libellous. I've always deplored that kind of coverage.'

'Then it wasn't you who said, "No publicity is bad publicity"?'

Happy to respond to what seemed to be a change of mood, he answered with a grin, 'What do you think?'

His smile showed the gleam of white, healthy teeth, formed deep creases each side of his mouth and filled his dark face with charm.

Very conscious of his sexual magnetism and hating him for it, Charlotte made an effort to smile back.

She found it easier than she had anticipated. It seemed she was a better actress than she had given herself credit for.

Rocked by that smile, he told her, 'I'm afraid my present relationship with the press leaves a lot to be desired. After being asked at a recent press conference what I thought of modern journalism, I stated my belief that some journalists not only embroider the truth but fabricate what they don't know. Since then they've been out for blood.'

'Are they lies?' The question was out before she could prevent it.

'Very often they are,' he said steadily. 'Though I don't pretend to live like a monk, most of their stories are just that. Stories. But, unfortunately, when dirt's thrown some of it's bound to stick.'

'But surely you were once the press's Golden Boy?'

'I was until I proved to be uncooperative… Which I can never accuse *you* of being.' Smoothly he changed the subject. 'I hope agreeing to make this transfer so soon didn't cause you too many problems?'

'No, not at all.'

'You're not leaving behind anyone special? A boyfriend, perhaps?'

'No.'

Only too pleased to have Sheering's report confirmed, Daniel queried, 'How did you manage with regard to your flat?'

'The flat is a rented one I share with an old school friend, so that was no problem.'

'Most people would have balked at being parted from their families this close to Christmas.'

Her voice under control she said, 'I have no family to share Christmas with.'

He waited.

When she failed to mention her stepbrother, Daniel wondered why. Even though he was her boss, he couldn't believe she lacked either the will or the courage to confront him.

Ready to tell her how much he regretted what had happened, to explain his part in it, he asked a number of careful questions, skirting round the family issue, giving her every chance to bring things into the open.

When she failed to do so he was forced to conclude that, for whatever reason, she had made up her mind to say nothing.

Though he himself would have preferred to confront the issue, if she *had* decided to leave the past behind then, for the time being at least, he would go along with that.

Charlotte, having answered his questions with at least outward composure, was feeling a little more sure of herself. Even so, she seemed unable to get her act together.

Though she knew she might never have this kind of opportunity again, and she should be making the most of it, she could think of nothing sparkling to say, no way to interest him.

When the silence began to stretch, reasonably satisfied with how things had gone so far, Daniel asked, 'Have you ever been to New York before?'

Relieved to move on to this new subject, she answered, 'No, I haven't, though I've always wanted to go.'

'I hope you'll enjoy the experience.'

'I'm sure I will.'

Then, seizing the chance to carry on with the conversation, 'What's it like, living in New York?'

'It's overcrowded, and the traffic is a nightmare. In summer it can be hot and dusty and airless, and in winter cold and bleak and snowy.

'In common with most cities it has its share of crime and deprivation and weirdos. But in the past it's always been alive and vibrant. Synonymous with exciting.

'These days it's like an old dog that, though it's been badly beaten, is still brave and beautiful. And you'll find that most New Yorkers are great. They have the same kind of indomitable spirit that Londoners do.

'I've always thought New York was a wonderful place to be, and I wouldn't want to live anywhere else.

'Having said that, however, I don't lose sight of the fact

that I'm one of the fortunate ones, with a home in a pleasant area and a chauffeur-driven car.

'When it's too hot and humid I can move out to the beaches on Long Island, and when it's miserable and slushy underfoot I can travel Upstate to the virgin snow of the Catskills.'

'It sounds idyllic.'

'As I say, I'm one of the lucky ones.'

When she said no more he steered the conversation towards the latest news.

Charlotte followed his lead and until they reached the airport, like polite strangers, they talked about what was happening in the world.

As the limousine drew up outside Departures, with a sinking heart Charlotte realized that her chance to make the right kind of impression on Daniel Wolfe was gone. As soon as the chauffeur had finished unloading their luggage she and her companion would no doubt part company.

The best she dared hope for was that she had made enough of an impact that once in New York he might possibly renew contact to ask how she was getting on.

But when, having smiled and thanked him for the lift, she said goodbye and prepared to go, he shook his head. 'Stick with me, Miss Michaels.'

'But I have to pick up my ticket.'

'That's all taken care of. We're both booked on the same plane.'

Before she had got over her amazement he had gathered her up and, a hand at her waist, swept her along with him as though she were his equal rather than his employee.

At five feet seven inches she was fairly tall for a woman, but he must be a minimum of six feet three inches, she guessed, and seemed even bigger because of the breadth of his shoulders.

Focused and powerful, he moved lithely and fast on the

balls of his feet, a tight mass of coiled energy, and she found herself almost trotting to keep up with his long strides.

Travelling with Daniel Wolfe, she soon found, was a totally new experience. VIP treatment smoothed their path and added immeasurably to their ease and convenience.

After being whisked through the formalities, they were served with a tray of excellent coffee before boarding the big jet and being shown to a pair of First Class seats.

Charlotte was staggered. Surely it hadn't happened by chance? She shot him a puzzled glance.

He raised a dark brow. 'Something wrong?'

'No…I just didn't think… I mean, I hadn't expected that we'd be on the same plane, let alone sitting together.'

His silvery eyes on her face, he queried mildly, 'I hope the prospect of having me sitting next to you during the flight doesn't seriously bother you?'

'N-no, of course not. I'm just surprised.'

'As we were travelling at the same time, I told my secretary to book adjacent seats. I found the thought of a little company welcome. I hope you do?'

'Very welcome,' Charlotte assured him with her most fetching smile.

So was the unaccustomed luxury.

Used to being crowded into economy, she was staggered by how very comfortable and spacious the First Class area was.

In spite of her tension, or maybe because of it, almost as soon as they were airborne she found herself having to stifle a yawn.

'Tired?' he queried, proving he missed nothing.

'I didn't get much sleep last night,' she admitted.

'Over-excited?'

'Probably.'

'Then why not have a little nap before lunch?'

She shook her head. 'I have been known to fall asleep in cars and buses, but never on planes.'

Taking off his jacket he queried, 'Any particular reason?'

Without intending to she found herself telling him the truth. 'I can't relax enough. I'm never really happy flying. My father was killed in a plane crash.'

'I'm sorry. How long ago was that?'

'Six years.'

'I'm sorry. And what about your mother?'

'My mother died when I was quite young and my father married again.'

'His dying like that must have been hard on both you and your stepmother.'

Her generous mouth tightening, she said shortly, 'My stepmother didn't care.'

'Oh?'

'She was playing around with another man when it happened.'

Her companion waited, his eyes on her face.

Though she had had no intention of revealing any more, Charlotte found herself saying, 'He was an oil company executive and barely a month after my father's funeral she married him and went to live in the Middle East.'

Knowing Tim Hunt must have been just a schoolboy at the time, Daniel waited for her to go on. But once again she said nothing about her stepbrother.

After a moment, he probed, 'I guess you were still at college?'

Wondering vexedly why she had told him so much, Charlotte answered briefly, 'Yes, I was.'

Seeing she didn't want to carry on the conversation and watching her smother another yawn, he said, 'Nap time, I think.'

He adjusted the angle of the seats so that they were reclining comfortably and gathered her close.

'Put your head on my shoulder.' He settled her head at the comfortable juncture between chest and shoulder, adding, as he might have done to a child, 'I'll keep you safe.'

For an instant everything seemed to stop—her heartbeat, her breathing, her very lifeblood—and she froze into stillness.

Then, with a kind of backlash, she felt an almost uncontrollable urge to tear herself away and cry *Keep your hands off me, you swine!*

But the last thing she must do was let her true feelings show. She had to play-act for all she was worth.

Though for the moment any acting ability seemed to have totally deserted her.

Recalling Carla's advice, she knew she should be snuggling against him, doing the 'wide-eyed and helpless' bit, but somehow she couldn't.

Breathing in the clean freshness of his shirt, the faint suggestion of shower-gel and the masculine scent of his aftershave, all she could do was stay quite still, every muscle in her body taut.

'Relax,' he urged softly.

Only too aware of his overpowering maleness, the firmness of bone and muscle beneath her cheek, the sureness and strength of his arm holding her, she knew it would be impossible to relax.

But after a while, with a weight of warmth and tiredness lying over her body like a cashmere shawl, her tension drained away and she slept.

When she finally stirred and resurfaced for a second or two she had no idea where she was, or who was holding her so closely.

'Feeling better, Miss Michaels...?' a pleasant male voice queried.

'Yes, thank you,' she mumbled.

Looking into forest-green eyes still dazed with sleep, he added, 'Or may I call you Charlotte…?'

'Please do,' she replied automatically as she gathered her wits and struggled to sit up.

His smile teasing, he said, 'Somehow, I feel that watching over you while you slept has moved our relationship on to a more…shall we say…*personal* footing.'

Flustered by the thought of Daniel Wolfe watching her sleep, she drew hastily away.

Removing his arm and readjusting the seats, he pursued, 'You must have been absolutely shattered. You've slept for almost two hours.'

A glance at her watch confirmed the truth of his statement. 'I—I'm sorry,' she stammered. 'I haven't been much company.'

In truth, he had enjoyed the chance to just hold her quietly and watch her sleeping face.

When Glenda, his younger sister, married and became a mother, she had once remarked how much time she and her husband had spent just *looking* at the cherished new arrival.

Finding it difficult to take his eyes off his companion, Daniel now knew exactly what his sister had meant.

Studying that glorious hair, the silky brows and thick, naturally-dark lashes that curled so enticingly, the pure curve of her cheek, he had felt a fierce desire.

Then noticing how, in repose, her soft mouth drooped a little at the corners, as though she'd forgotten how to be happy, he had felt an odd kind of tenderness mingling with desire.

Now seeing her look of genuine concern he shook his head. 'There's nothing to be sorry for, I do assure you.'

Tucking in a tendril of silky, red-gold hair that had escaped from its neat coil, Charlotte sighed inwardly. Though he sounded quite laid back about the lack of company she was vexed with herself. She should have been using that time to amuse him, rather than just sleeping.

Once they reached New York and went their separate ways, it would be too late...

'About ready for some lunch?' His voice broke into her thoughts.

Finding herself unexpectedly hungry, she nodded.

'What do you fancy?' He handed her a menu that bore little resemblance to the kind of airline food she had been served in the past.

Seeing her hesitate, he asked, 'Something wrong?'

'I'm just bowled over by the choice,' she admitted. 'I usually travel economy class.'

He grinned. 'Oh yes, I remember it well.'

'You do?' She failed to hide her surprise.

With a kind of wry self-mockery he told her, 'After graduating, to see what I was made of, I spent a couple of years working my way round the globe. At times cash was so tight that even those ubiquitous plastic containers were welcome...'

While they ate a leisurely lunch followed by coffee and brandy they talked about his travels and the various places he'd visited.

'Have you travelled much?' he asked at length.

'Not as much as I would have wished.'

'Even though you dislike flying?'

'I wouldn't have let that stop me. At one time I'd planned to go round the world when I finished college, but...' She stopped speaking abruptly.

'But?'

'I had commitments.' She still felt unbearably desolate and sad when she thought of Tim. Poor Tim. And it was all this man's fault.

A fresh wave of anger and hatred shook her.

Watching her, Daniel waited.

When she said nothing he queried carefully, 'Is there anywhere in particular you'd still like to go?'

Taking a deep steadying breath she answered, 'Quite a lot of places. But until earlier this year Carla—the girl I share the flat with—has been lighting candles for my financial status.'

'It doesn't sound as if we're paying you enough.'

'As I said, I had commitments.'

It seemed as if Sheering had been right when he suggested that Charlotte had been supporting her stepbrother, Daniel thought, and once again he waited, hoping she would go on.

But her face had that still, controlled look he was coming to recognize and, sighing inwardly, he decided to back off and change the subject.

Leaving the more emotive topics, he began to talk about international finance and how it affected current business interests.

After a moment, appearing cool and collected now, she joined in and held her own in a conversation that, though general, was deep and wide-ranging.

He moved easily from money issues and world trade to global warming and the preservation of natural resources. All the time testing her knowledge, seeking her reaction, asking her opinion, which, greatly to her surprise, often seemed to coincide with his.

If they touched on a subject that she was more familiar with than he was he saluted her superior knowledge. Generously.

Used to being talked down to by the men on her team who seemed to think brains and beauty were incompatible, she found it stimulating to be taken seriously and treated as an equal.

By the time they reached New York and came in to land

at busy JFK Airport she had almost forgotten her reason
for being there.

Almost.

Once again, with a light but firm hand at her waist,
Daniel Wolfe took charge of everything. In no time at all,
it seemed, the formalities were completed and their luggage
was being ferried to a waiting limousine by a smartly uniformed chauffeur.

Instead of being dull and damp, as it had been in London,
to Charlotte's surprise there was a fresh cover of snow.
Overhead the sky was a cloudless cornflower-blue, and the
sun shone coldly bright.

As they drove through Queens, which seemed to be
mainly residential, she queried, 'How far is it?'

'About fifteen miles to mid-Manhattan. It'll take about
an hour, depending on the traffic.'

Though aware that she should be using the time to advantage Charlotte could think of nothing else to say, and
once again very conscious of the man by her side she
looked resolutely through the car window.

For his part, his first surging excitement now leashed by
his better judgement, Daniel was content to simply have
her by his side.

Earlier, on the plane, the urge to hold her in his arms
had been so great that he had thrown caution to the winds.

He had felt her momentary withdrawal, her tenseness
and, expecting the worst, had braced himself for an open
rejection.

When it hadn't come he had been both pleased and puzzled. Either she had decided to forgive and forget or she
was playing some deep game of her own.

Whichever, it seemed that, in the short term at least, life
was going to be far from dull.

they reached New York and came in to land

CHAPTER THREE

As THEY approached Manhattan, though Charlotte had seen enough pictures to make it reasonably familiar, she still caught her breath at the sight of the city decked all in sparkling white.

'Isn't it wonderful?' she exclaimed.

'I think so,' he agreed.

Her reason for being there momentarily forgotten, she turned to him in excitement. 'I thought I knew what to expect, but I hadn't imagined anything quite like this.'

Pleased and relieved that she liked his city, he said, 'New York has so many different faces, so many moods, that it's always able to surprise even the people who call it home. That's one of the reasons I enjoy living here.'

His comment reminded her of something she still wasn't sure about, and she asked, 'Perhaps you can tell me where *I'll* be living? Mr Telford mentioned a company flat, but I've no idea where it is.'

'The company flat is at our headquarters in the Lloyd Wolfe building, which is situated Uptown on Central Park East.'

'Is that where you live?'

'No. I live in Lower Manhattan.'

'Oh!' It would have suited her purpose better if he'd been living in the same building.

'You sound disappointed.'

He seemed able to pick up the slightest inflection she thought uncomfortably, and hastened to deny. 'Not at all. It's just that for some reason I'd expected you to have a penthouse on Fifth Avenue.'

'I did for a while but it didn't really suit me, so I moved... Sure you're not disappointed?'

'No, of course not. Why should I be?' Then, seeing he was far from convinced, she added, 'I'm just surprised. I can't imagine anyone not enjoying living on Fifth Avenue.'

'I did, in a way, but as well as being relatively run-of-the-mill the penthouse always seemed a touch impersonal, like living in a hotel.

'Now I have a house that's different, as well as being very personal. It's in an area usually referred to as The Villages.'

'The Villages?' she echoed uncertainly.

'They're a collection of neighbourhoods just west of Broadway.'

'Isn't that quite a way from your headquarters?'

'Not too far, as the crow flies.'

'Do you go in every day?'

'Yes, unless I'm away on business.'

'And you don't find the traffic a pain?'

'It can be, of course, but a chauffeur-driven car does a great deal to mitigate it.'

'Is that where I'll be working?'

'Yes.'

'Well, if I'm living on the spot *I* won't have far to travel,' she remarked with a smile.

'Unfortunately, because of the very short notice, the accommodation there is still occupied.'

'Oh...'

'It should be vacated in the next two or three days, and then you'll be able to move in and get settled before Christmas.

'In the meantime, I thought you could stay at my place.'

'Stay at your place?' she echoed, knowing she should be pleased, but momentarily horrified and sounding it.

'Like most big cities, New York can be a bit lonely and

unnerving,' he went on smoothly, 'especially if you're on your own and don't know the ropes. So, rather than book you into a hotel, I thought you could have the small self-contained suite that my housekeeper used to occupy… Unless, of course, you have any serious objections to living under my roof for a short time?'

Recovering a little, and somewhat reassured that he'd described it as a *self-contained* suite, she stammered, 'W-well… No.'

Delighted by the relative lack of opposition, he remarked quizzically, 'I thought the press might have managed to convince you that no woman is safe when I'm around?'

She didn't need convincing, Charlotte thought bitterly, she already knew that he was a ruthless womanizer.

Managing to look amused, she said coolly, 'I don't believe *all* I read.'

'In that case, we'll call it settled.'

'Thank you.'

'It's my pleasure, I assure you.' He smiled into her eyes, a personal communication that emphasized the fact that he was already interested in her as a woman rather than just an employee.

Returning his smile, Charlotte reflected with a surge of triumph that things seemed to be going her way. Thanks to the company flat being occupied, she might have several more days of what should be fairly close contact to try and increase that interest.

His grey eyes were still looking into hers and, afraid he might read her thoughts, she said quickly, 'Won't you tell me about The Villages?'

'They're wonderful places to live, with first-class restaurants, good theatre and a great variety of night-life. The best known is undoubtedly Greenwich Village, with Washington Square as its heart…'

He talked knowledgeably about The Villages and their

history until they reached an area where the streets no longer conformed to the rigid grid system and had a friendly, small-town feel to them.

The main thoroughfare, with its boutiques and cafés, its bookstores and art galleries, was busy and bustling with Christmas shoppers.

Snow was piled along the edges of the sidewalks, white and uneven, like miniature mountain ranges and, despite the sunshine, a row of icicles hung from an upper storey windowsill.

The stores were bright with decorations and tinsel. In one window a red-coated Santa rode on a loaded sleigh pulled by prancing reindeer, while in another elves and furry woodland creatures tied a green scarf around the neck of a carrot-nosed snowman.

Leaving the main shopping centre and most of the traffic behind them, they reached a quieter residential area and turned left into Carver Street.

A cul-de-sac lined with bare snowy trees and elegant brownstones, Carver Street meandered a little, like an amiable drunk.

At the end, standing detached and fronting on to the street, was a small three-storey house with a steeply-pitched roof and overhanging eaves.

It was built of pink and blue bricks in a herringbone pattern and its garden was surrounded by a high brick wall.

Five steps, an iron handrail on their right, led up to a central front door with a black wrought iron lantern hanging over it.

On either side of the door were two long windows with rounded tops and small square panes of uneven glass that picked up the light. Above the polished brass knocker, shaped like a lily, hung a holly wreath with a scarlet bow.

The whole thing was so totally unexpected that Charlotte wanted to pinch herself to make sure she wasn't dreaming.

'This is where I live,' Daniel told her. 'As you can see, it's really quite small.'

In a city like New York this charming little house should have appeared totally incongruous, an anachronism, but somehow its aura of calm serenity, its air of *belonging* here, made it look as much at home as the Statue of Liberty.

Stopping by the kerb, the chauffeur sprang to open the car door.

'Thank you, Perkins.' Daniel stepped out first into several inches of snow.

Turning to take Charlotte's hand, he said, 'Mind you don't slip.'

She heeded his warning and descended carefully.

The sun had disappeared, leaving a sky of icy pearl, and the air was decidedly chill.

Conditions underfoot serving as a good excuse, he put an arm around her waist while they crossed the sidewalk and climbed the steps.

Just for a moment it gave her the perilous illusion of being cared for.

Taking an ornate iron key from his pocket, he opened the door and, standing aside, ushered her in. 'Welcome to The Lilies,' he said with grave courtesy.

'Thank you.' She stepped over the threshold and wiped her feet on the doormat.

Ducking his head to follow her, he felt a surge of pure elation. The woman he'd wanted for so long was in his house at last and he couldn't wait to get her into his bed.

But he couldn't afford to rush things a warning voice reminded him. In the past it had never mattered if a woman refused—there was always another one in the offing—but Charlotte Michaels was different, and this time it *did* matter.

As Daniel closed the door behind them Charlotte gazed around the living-room with unfeigned delight. It was old-fashioned and utterly charming, with period wallpaper and white plaster cornices decorated with sheaves of lilies.

The minimum of furniture, all of it glowing with the patina of age, stood on dark oak polished floorboards and on the right a small graceful staircase curved up to the second floor.

A bright fire burnt in the grate of a purply-blue ceramic fireplace adorned with garlands of white lilies, and a thick white sheepskin rug lay in front of the hearth.

Grouped nearby was a trug-shaped log basket, a hexagonal coffee table, a single wing-backed chair and a settee covered in dull gold velvet and piled with cushions.

Various other rugs and curtains tied back with bows picked up and echoed the indigo-blue of the fire-surround.

Between the long windows a tall beautifully decorated Christmas tree with a star on top stood in a tub. It was a fresh one and Charlotte could smell the pungent scent of pine needles and resin.

The ceilings were low, as were the doorways, and to Charlotte's fascinated eyes everything seemed to be slightly scaled down.

It put her in mind of a dolls' house.

She glanced at the man standing by her side.

Someone as big and masculine as Daniel Wolfe should have looked completely out of place in this pretty little house. But somehow he didn't. He looked at home, happy here, as if he belonged.

She was about to make a remark to that effect when a door opened at the far end of the room and a short middle-aged woman with apple-red cheeks and a mass of frizzy grey hair appeared.

Dressed in neat navy trousers, a scarlet sweater, a pair of wellington boots and a man's cap, she was carrying a length of twine and a pair of scissors.

If she had been wearing the right kind of hat she could have passed for a cheery garden gnome.

Catching Daniel Wolfe's eye, Charlotte saw by the twinkle in it that they were on the same wavelength. Somehow that fleeting moment of intimacy left her strangely shaken.

The newcomer beamed at Daniel, her face round and plump, with no angles or bone-structure visible.

'Sorry I wasn't here to let you in. I'd gone into the garden to tie up the plants that the snow was weighing down. I didn't realize you were back until I saw Perkins putting the car away. What kind of flight did you have?'

'Excellent, thanks.' Then gravely, 'Charlotte, this is my housekeeper, Mrs Morgan...'

Charlotte smiled and said, 'Hello.'

'Kate, this is Miss Michaels.'

'Pleased to meet you, Miss Michaels,' Kate responded breezily. 'Everything's ready for you, if you'd like me to take you up?'

'I'll show Miss Michaels around if you want to get off,' Daniel suggested. 'You must have plenty to do.'

'That I have,' the housekeeper said. 'I haven't finished my Christmas shopping yet, and everywhere's so crowded... Now, is there anything you'd like before I go?'

'A pot of tea, perhaps.'

'The kettle's just on the boil, so I'll make one on my way out.' With a smile that encompassed them both, she bustled away.

'There's not a lot to see,' Daniel remarked to Charlotte, 'but I may as well show you around downstairs before we have our tea.'

He opened double doors to the left. 'This is the diningroom, though it's hardly ever used these days. When I'm at home I prefer to eat in the kitchen...'

The dining-room had the same kind of ceramic fireplace,

a ticking clock on the mantelpiece and a neatly ordered air. All the furniture and fittings belonged to a past century.

'And next to it is my library-cum-study…'

It was an attractive book-lined room, with comfortable-looking furniture and a log-filled fireplace. The only obvious concession to the twenty-first century was a range of state-of-the-art computer equipment that sat on a leather-topped desk.

'Apart from the kitchen that's about it,' he told her cheerfully. 'As I said, it's not very big.'

Leading her through to the rear of the house, he indicated a flight of plain wooden stairs that ran up from a small inner hall. 'That used to be the servants' staircase.'

'There doesn't seem to be much room for servants.' She spoke the thought aloud.

'At one time the whole of the top floor and some of the attic rooms were servants' quarters. Since I moved in they've been standing empty, or used for storage.'

'But you still have servants.'

'Only two.'

She frowned. Though this house, unique as it was, must have cost a small fortune, Daniel Wolfe appeared to live very simply. Nothing she had read in the papers about his lifestyle tallied in the slightest with what she was learning firsthand.

'Apart from Kate,' he went on, accompanying her into the kitchen, 'there's just the chauffeur and he has a flat over what used to be a stable block but is now garages…'

The kitchen was neat and cosy with an oak table and chairs and a black range in which a fire burnt brightly. At first glance it seemed to date back a hundred years, but Charlotte soon realized that built-in unobtrusively was every labour-saving device imaginable.

Drawn up in front of the leaping flames were a couple

of easy chairs and waiting on a low table a tray set with a china teapot and cups and saucers.

Mrs Morgan had been as good as her word.

'Ready for some tea?' Daniel enquired.

As she answered, 'Please,' with a sense of shock she realized that for the first time they were quite alone together and felt an almost overwhelming desire to run.

'Milk and sugar?'

'Just milk, please.'

When she continued to hover uneasily he suggested, 'Why don't you sit down?'

She obeyed and, taking the seat beside her, he began to pour.

While she watched his lean well-shaped hands deftly doing what she had always thought of as a feminine task she found herself marvelling at their sheer masculinity.

They were strong hands, with long fingers and neatly-trimmed nails. Skilful hands, no doubt. Hands that knew how to pleasure a woman.

She shivered as she imagined them moving delicately over her naked body; imagined what delight they would bring as they stroked and caressed and teased…

'There we go.' He handed her a cup.

With a mumbled, 'Thank you,' she looked up unwarily and met his glance.

Grey eyes gleaming, he smiled a little as though he was privy to her erotic fantasy.

She tried to tell herself that he *couldn't* be, but she felt sure that he was a great deal too experienced not to know naked lust when he saw it, and she felt her face start to flame.

Damn, oh damn! If he hadn't already guessed what she was thinking, he almost certainly would now.

Scarlet as a poppy, looking anywhere but at him, she

wondered in horror how she could have let herself think that way about a man she hated?

It wasn't like her to fantasize about sex. Just the opposite, in fact.

As Carla had once remarked, she was as repressed and inhibited, as self-restrained, as anyone who wasn't narrow-minded could possibly be.

'If you don't soon get yourself a sex life', the other girl had added, 'you'll be a shrivelled up virgin long before you're thirty'.

Perhaps it had been that threat that had made her start to go out with Peter. But it hadn't worked. The more he had clung to her, the more she had withdrawn. He had called her cold and uncaring, accused her of being incapable of passion.

She had made a determined attempt to loosen up, but even with an engagement ring on her finger she had found it impossible.

Now here she was, picturing herself in bed with Daniel Wolfe!

Pushing the hateful thought away, Charlotte tried hard to regain her composure while she sipped her tea and looked around her.

On either side of a sturdy back door there were long windows with deep sills and frosted panes that overlooked a garden encircled by mature trees.

On a smooth expanse of snow-covered lawn she could make out the tracks of some small animal and somewhere close at hand a bird was singing.

A terrace, flanked by terracotta pots that in summer would be full of geraniums, ran the length of the house, while to one side stood what appeared to be a built-in bar-becue

What was left of the daylight was fading rapidly, and

even as she watched dusk began to press against the outside
of the glass like grey mist.

The garden, and the room, lit only by the flickering fire,
could well have belonged to a cottage in rural England.

She put her cup and saucer down and broke the silence
to remark, 'You said you had a house that was different,
but I hadn't dreamt it would be anything like this.'

Turning to look at her squarely, Daniel asked, 'And do
you approve?'

'Oh, yes, I do. It's lovely! It puts me in mind of a dolls'
house.'

He smiled. 'I know just what you mean.'

'It must be unique.'

The fire glow gleaming in his eyes and turning his handsome face ruddy, he said with quiet satisfaction, 'I believe
it is.'

'Do you know its history?'

'Oh, yes. Over a hundred and fifty years ago it was built
by John Lloyd, an eminent English architect, for his mistress, Lily Bosiney. She was on the stage and, a noted
beauty with glorious red hair, the toast of London Town.

'It seems that their love affair was a very passionate one
and he wanted to marry her. But he already had a wife,
Florence, whom he'd married out of necessity when they
were both very young. Florence had never been particularly
strong, and after the birth of their daughter, Elizabeth, she
became a semi-invalid.

'When John Lloyd decided to join the branch of his family who were already in the States, and had been for over
a generation, he begged Lily to follow him.

'She said that she would if he agreed to leave his wife
and child in London.

'He was unwilling to desert his family but he couldn't
bear to lose Lily, so he promised that if she came he would
build her her very own house. Which he did. Lily loved

the flowers she'd been called after, hence the decorations, and the name of the house.'

Charlotte sighed. 'What a romantic story... And was she happy here?'

'She was for a year or two, but then it seems she got tired of snatched meetings and lonely nights. Tired of sharing the man she loved with a woman who had a much stronger claim on his time and attention.

'When Lloyd once again refused to leave his wife, Lily walked out. Knowing how strong their love was, he thought it was just a gesture and she would come back. But she didn't.

'He hired detectives and made every effort to trace her, both in New York and London, but without success. She appeared to have vanished off the face of the earth.

'Shortly after, when his wife died, he left young Elizabeth with her doting governess and came to live at The Lilies, hoping against hope that his Lily would come back.'

'And did she?'

'I'm afraid not. John Lloyd lived here alone for almost forty years, until he died.

'Times were changing, and to prevent developers buying *her* house and tearing it down he willed it to Save Our Heritage, a local preservation society of which he was a founder member.

'A couple of years back I bought it from them.'

'Oh? I'm surprised they parted with it.'

Raising a dark brow, he asked quizzically, 'You mean you're surprised they trusted me?'

She met his eyes and, feeling the full force of his magnetism, suddenly found herself breathless.

Angered by his effect on her, she said, 'Well you're known to be a hard-headed businessman.'

'I can't imagine they would have trusted me if that's all I'd been…'

Remembering the newspaper stories about his philanthropy, she remarked derisively, 'No doubt you'd been a very generous benefactor?'

'You could put it that way,' he agreed evenly. 'But there was a lot more to it than that.'

'Really?'

'Having bought up several historical properties and overstretched themselves, the Society was having a struggle to keep going—'

'So you rode up like a knight on a white charger to rescue them?'

'I offered to buy The Lilies and, after I'd met the Society's asking price and agreed to certain conditions, the sale went through.'

'Money talks, as my father used to say.'

'I can't deny that. Though it's not the be all and end all.'

'It's usually enough.'

'Money alone wouldn't have been enough in this particular instance.'

'You had to use your charm?' she asked sweetly.

He gave her a glinting look. 'Fortunately, I didn't have to rely on that rather sparse commodity. It was the fact that my great-great-grandfather had built The Lilies that made the Society decide in my favour.'

'John Lloyd was your great-great-grandfather?'

'Yes. His daughter married her American cousin, Joshua Wolfe, and became Elizabeth Lloyd Wolfe.'

Of course, she remembered him mentioning that his headquarters were in the Lloyd Wolfe building.

'But perhaps you still think they were wrong to let me have the house?' he pursued.

'No, of course not.'

Furious with herself, Charlotte bit her lip. Though from

the first he hadn't treated her as his employee, for the moment at least she should be treating him as her employer.

So what on earth was she thinking of, sneering at a man who was at once her boss and her host? A man she had been hoping to charm.

She should have listened and smiled politely instead of letting her hostility show.

There was only one thing she could do and she did it. 'I'm sorry. I shouldn't have said what I did.'

'There's no need to apologize. You're entitled to voice your opinion.'

She shook her head. 'Considering I'm your guest it wasn't very gracious of me. And at the very least I should have waited to hear the facts.'

'Please don't worry about it.'

Then, apparently determined to change the subject, he remarked, 'With the time difference you must be getting tired?'

Grateful that he hadn't taken offence and feeling the need to be alone to marshal her forces, she seized on the excuse. 'I am rather.'

'The trouble is, if you go to bed too early it's difficult to get into the right sleep pattern.

'May I suggest that when you've unpacked you put your feet up for an hour or so? Then I'll take you out to dinner and show you Fifth Avenue by night.'

'Thank you, that sounds wonderful. But are you sure you have the time?'

'Quite sure.'

'And there won't be a problem? I mean…' She hesitated and stopped.

'You mean have I a current lady friend who's likely to object?'

'Well, yes…'

'Then the answer's no.'

The rush of relief she felt seemed disproportionate, but she told herself that she was pleased simply because it removed one major obstacle from her path.

'Now, shall I show you up?'

Rising to his feet and flicking on lights as they went, though being in a city it wasn't really dark, he ushered her across the living-room and up the main staircase to a polished landing.

'Here, at the front of the house, is the master bedroom...' He opened the door into a good-sized, simply furnished room.

His room. Though everything was neat there was no mistaking the signs of male occupation.

Making no effort to go in, she stood on the landing and looked along the length of Carver Street, with its glowing street lamps and black and white skeletal trees etched against the evening sky.

The snowy scene with the lighted brownstones, many of their windows and doors hung with festive decorations, would have made a good Christmas card, she found herself thinking.

'And this—' leading her across the landing, Daniel opened another door '—is your suite. It looks over the garden.'

Her suite comprised of a small sitting-room, a bedroom and a bathroom that, in spite of appearing to be a charming period-piece, boasted every modern convenience.

The two main rooms had dainty antique furniture, dark oak floorboards and tiny fireplaces. Though the grates were empty, apart from piled up pine cones, the rooms were comfortably warm, which suggested discreet central-heating.

On the high double bed there was a patchwork quilt, faded by much washing, while the rich colours of the wallpaper and rugs had been mellowed by time and sunshine. It was serenely beautiful.

Though she had almost forgotten what it was like to be happy, she knew instinctively that this was a house she could be happy in.

If it wasn't for its owner.

Seeing the shadow fall over her face, he asked, 'I hope you like it?'

'Yes, I do,' she answered simply. 'Thank you.'

Satisfied by her unmistakable sincerity, he said, 'Then I'll leave you to get settled in. I'll give you a knock in a couple of hours, shall I?'

'Please.'

He went quietly, closing the door behind him.

Her luggage was waiting and she unpacked swiftly, setting aside clean underwear and a midnight-blue cocktail dress with a matching jacket.

At the bottom of her case was a warm evening cloak with a big loose hood that Carla had bullied her into buying and which she had never really expected to wear. Now she shook it out and placed it over a chair.

Stifling a yawn, she took off her suit and blouse and, setting her small travel alarm clock to give her plenty of time to shower and change, climbed into bed and turned off the light.

Though she was very tired, with so much to think about, she hadn't expected to sleep, and it was a shock when the alarm went off almost before she had closed her eyes.

Fumbling for the light switch, she peered at the clock and was surprised to see that she had actually slept for more than an hour and a half.

All she wanted to do at that moment was turn over and go back to sleep, but soon Daniel Wolfe would be knocking at her door.

She got out of bed and, like a walking zombie, made her

way to the bathroom. When she had splashed her face with cold water she felt a lot better.

In less than fifteen minutes she had showered and dressed and was practically ready. She was fastening pearl drops to her neat earlobes when his knock came.

Picking up her cloak and bag, she opened the door.

He was wearing immaculate evening clothes and looked so powerfully virile and attractive that she stood rooted to the spot, her heart starting to race.

His eyes travelled slowly, appreciatively, over her from head to toe and back again. 'You look a million dollars. That colour really suits you.'

As they descended the stairs, her whole body still quivering from his scrutiny, she asked huskily, 'I hope it's dressy enough? It's all I have with me.'

With a smile that reached his grey eyes and warmed them into life, he said, 'It's perfect. I'll be the envy of every man who sees you.'

In the living-room he paused to put her cloak around her shoulders and pick up his own overcoat before escorting her outside.

The limousine was drawn up at the kerb, the chauffeur standing smartly by to open the door.

It was so cold that their breath made white puffs of mist on the air.

As soon as they were settled in the warmth and luxury of the big car Daniel slid aside the glass panel and said to the chauffeur, 'We'll be dining at La Havane but we're in no particular hurry. I'd like Miss Michaels to see Fifth Avenue, so if you can go that way…?'

'Certainly, sir.'

Daniel turned to Charlotte. 'Would you prefer to be set down outside the restaurant or would you like to walk a block or two first?'

'I'd like to walk.'

'In that case, Perkins, you can drop us off just before we get to 50th Street.'

Though very aware of the muscular thigh almost brushing hers, Charlotte made an effort to relax and enjoy the fabulous night-time drive through the city.

Watching her half-averted face, and resisting the temptation to lean forward and kiss her nape, from time to time Daniel pointed out landmarks.

'On the right is Madison Square Park... And in a little while, on the left, we'll be passing the Empire State Building...'

Fifth Avenue, with its sumptuous shop windows and dazzling festive displays, was all and more than she had hoped for. Thronged with people and traffic, it had an air of exuberance, an ambience that surpassed all her expectations.

To add to the Christmassy feel, a few white flakes were beginning to drift down and, having always loved snow, she gave a little murmur of pleasure.

As they approached 50th Street Perkins asked, 'About here, sir?'

Turning to his companion, Daniel observed, 'It's starting to snow again. Are you quite sure you want to walk?'

'Yes, please.'

'This will do fine, thanks, Perkins. Don't bother to get out. I'll let you know what time we want to be picked up.'

As soon as the car drew to a halt, Daniel shrugged on his overcoat and, jumping out, offered Charlotte his hand.

She took it reluctantly, his touch making every nerve-ending tingle, and followed him on to the sidewalk where the passage of many feet had virtually cleared the carpet of snow.

Turning to her, he lifted the big loose hood and settled it into place over her bright hair before tucking her arm through his.

Full of excitement, and a rather nervous anticipation,

Charlotte mentally girded herself for the evening that lay ahead.

In only one day, with luck on her side, she had achieved more than she could ever have dared hope for. If only that luck would stay with her, soon she might be able to return home satisfied that she had done a little towards avenging Tim's death.

CHAPTER FOUR

'FIRST we'll take a look at St Patrick's Cathedral, usually known as St Pat's, and then go on to see the Rockefeller Center tree, shall we?' Daniel asked.

She nodded breathlessly.

His dark head bare, his free hand thrust deep into his coat pocket, they began to walk in the direction of the magnificent cathedral.

When Charlotte had gazed her fill they angled across the street and strolled along with a throng of other sightseers to the massive Rockefeller Center.

'The complex covers twenty-two acres and has nineteen buildings,' Daniel told her.

As they drew near the plaza she exclaimed, 'Oh, an open-air skating rink! Is it always there?'

He shook his head. 'Only from October to April. In the warmer months the rink is transformed into the Summer Garden Restaurant. Both of which are presided over by Prometheus.'

'It's amazing,' she breathed, gazing at the huge golden statue.

'Eighteen foot, but dwarfed by the tree.'

Set up near the rink, where skaters carved icy circles, was a giant spruce. Encircling its base were barrel stays as large as mill wheels and near the top it was tethered to four adjacent buildings by thick guy wires.

Without warning Daniel took her hand, sending a tingle of awareness through her entire body. Finding it cold, in a curiously intimate gesture he returned both hands to the warmth of his pocket.

Her breathing suddenly becoming shallow and uneven, she tried to concentrate on the tree.

It was wonderfully decorated with strings of lights and baubles. A silver star gleamed on top and at ground level a bevy of glittering gold and silver angels lined up to guard it.

The whole scene was magical.

As she stood entranced snowflakes began to swirl around them like handfuls of confetti thrown at a wedding, settling on her hood and Daniel's dark hair.

She could have lingered indefinitely but after a while, breaking the spell, he said, 'We'd better be moving. Otherwise you'll start to get cold.'

They had only gone a few yards when a female voice cried, 'Why, Daniel, how lovely to see you!'

A beautiful dark-haired girl stood blocking their way. She was gazing at Daniel like a worshipper before a shrine.

'It's nice to see you,' Daniel said. His greeting was friendly without being enthusiastic. 'How are you, Maria?'

'I'm very well, thank you.' Then, reproachfully, 'I was hoping you'd accept Daddy's invitation to dinner the other night.'

'As I explained to your father, I had a business trip coming up.'

'But you're home again now, so you will join our Christmas house party, won't you?'

'I'm sorry, that's not possible.'

Her face fell. 'Then at least promise you'll come to our Christmas Eve get-together.'

'I'm afraid I can't promise.'

'Why not?'

'I may go Upstate for the holiday.'

'If you change your plans…?'

'I'll let you know.' He smiled politely, nodded to her

escort, who had stayed in the background, and led Charlotte away.

'An ex-girlfriend?' she queried when they were out of earshot. 'Or a would-be girlfriend?'

'Neither. Maria is the daughter of a business acquaintance.'

'She's in love with you.' The words were out before Charlotte could prevent them.

He slanted her a glance before asking evenly, 'Do I detect a note of censure?'

'Love hurts.'

'In all fairness, I must point out that I did nothing to encourage her. In any case, it's just a crush,' he added dismissively.

'Which you're careful not to take advantage of?'

'I'd be very much to blame if I did. Maria's just a child. She's barely eighteen.'

Janice had been only a year older, but it hadn't stopped him seducing her.

All her previous pleasure swamped by the reminder, Charlotte clenched her teeth and walked on through a night that had suddenly lost its magic.

La Havane was situated on the top floor of the sumptuous Conway Building and they stepped out of the elevator into a marble foyer that, to Charlotte, looked like an extravagant film set.

'Mr Wolfe, how nice to see you again.' They were welcomed by a man in immaculate evening dress. As their outdoor things were whisked away by one of his waiters he added genially, 'Gaston will be here in a moment to show you to your table.'

'Daniel, so you're back!' A tall, nice-looking young man with fine fair hair detached himself from a small party of businessmen who were just arriving and came over to them.

His sparkling blue eyes straying to Charlotte with frank curiosity, he added, 'How was the London trip?'

Looking as though the advent of the other man wasn't particularly welcome, Daniel answered briefly, 'Fine, thanks.'

'Will you be in tomorrow?'

'Apart from the finance meeting on the twenty-third, I'm not planning to come in until after Christmas, unless there are any problems.'

'Shouldn't be. The Smithson deal went off OK, and at present there's nothing much else that's dicey.'

His eyes straying to Charlotte once more, the newcomer lingered.

Good manners demanding it, Daniel made the introduction rather curtly. 'Charlotte, I'd like you to meet my cousin, Richard Shirland, who is also my Chief Executive Officer...

'Richard, this is Miss Michaels from our London headquarters.'

'How do you do?' Liking him on sight, Charlotte held out her hand with a smile.

Almost visibly reeling from her smile, Richard shook the proffered hand. 'I'm very pleased to meet you, Miss Michaels. I wish all out replacement staff were so decorative.'

It was said so ingenuously that, rather than being smarmy, she found the compliment charming.

'If you come straight to my office on Monday morning,' he added, 'I'll be pleased to show you around personally—'

'Miss Michaels won't be starting work on Monday morning,' Daniel broke in.

Without taking his eyes off Charlotte, Richard agreed, 'Of course. I suppose you'll want time to get settled in. As we'll be in the same building, if you need a hand just give me a ring.'

'Thank you. That's very kind of you.'

His friendliness and enthusiasm put her in mind of a Labrador puppy she had owned as a young child.

Clearly smitten, he suggested eagerly, 'Perhaps, as you're new to New York, I could take you out for a spot of lunch tomorrow? I'll give you a ring in the morning, shall I?'

'Thank you, but I—'

His displeasure barely concealed, Daniel said repressively, 'As the company apartment is occupied, Miss Michaels is staying with me for a few days.'

'I didn't realize the apartment was still occupied. In fact, I—'

Seeing the *maître d'* was approaching, Daniel cut his cousin off short. 'If you'll excuse us, our table's waiting.'

A hand cupping Charlotte's elbow, he was about to hurry her away when Richard Shirland called, 'If you *do* find you need help of any kind, Miss Michaels, just let me know.'

'Thank you.' She gave him a quick, grateful smile.

The *maître d'*, having inclined his head and greeted Daniel by name, turned to lead them through to the restaurant proper.

As they followed, glancing up at her companion surreptitiously, Charlotte saw that his jaw was tight and his dark brows were drawn together in a frown.

She hoped very much that his annoyance was caused by his cousin's only too obvious interest in her, and could be put down to jealousy.

Every instinct told her that it was so, but she mustn't count her chickens.

The dining area, which was quietly sumptuous, had a white and gold decor and wonderful panoramic views of the Manhattan skyline. It also had more than a touch of nineteen-thirties-style glamour.

On a dais at the far end of the room an orchestra was playing an old Cole Porter tune.

Widely spaced tables, separated by banks of flowers, radiated like the spokes of a wheel around the hub of a highly-polished dance floor, while on the perimeter were some discreetly-placed booths.

Finding they were shown to one of the more secluded booths, Charlotte wondered if Daniel usually brought his women here, and decided he probably did.

That impression was heightened when, as soon as they were seated, the wine waiter arrived with two crystal flutes and a bottle of vintage champagne in an ice bucket. After giving the bottle a twirl or two he eased out the cork with a satisfying pop and carefully poured the smoking wine.

When he had replaced it and gone Daniel raised his glass and, looking at his companion, toasted, 'Here's to us and getting to know each other better.'

No one had ever looked at her quite that way, at her face, her hair, into her eyes. Looked at her as if he couldn't get enough of her.

That look left her in no doubt that he *wanted* her.

But it had to be more than that.

Smiling brilliantly at him, she took a sip of the cool, crisp champagne, wrinkling her small nose at the bubbles.

'You're absolutely enchanting,' he said softly.

'I bet you say the same to all your women.'

'You make it sound as though there are hordes of them,' he objected quizzically.

'What about all the different women you're seen with in the newspapers?'

'I can't deny that I've taken quite a few women out, but—'

'Taken quite a few women out? Is that a euphemism?'

'For what?'

'For taking them to bed.'

He grinned ruefully. 'I've found that from time to time, when my partner is of the same mind, safe sex on a no-strings-involved, purely recreational basis, seems to work.'

'So it's all quite casual and cold-blooded?'

'I wouldn't say *cold-blooded*.'

'But you simply love them and leave them—' she felt oddly certain no woman had ever left him '—and the queue keeps moving?'

He gave a mock sigh. 'It seems I can't win. If I deny that I can see I'm going to be accused of keeping a harem.'

'You mean you don't?' She glanced at him from beneath long curly lashes, consciously flirting with him now.

'Afraid not. No matter what some sections of the press might try and make people believe, there haven't been all that many women, and never more than one at a time.'

Her half-smile teasing, she said, 'I thought perhaps you'd found a use for the top floor rooms you talked about earlier.'

Leaning forward to refill her glass, he told her, 'I've lived at The Lilies for quite some time now, and until you came today there's only ever been one other woman staying there.'

A strange constriction in her chest, Charlotte was wondering how special this other woman had been, when he added solemnly, 'And can you really see Mrs Morgan as harem material?'

She gave a little choke of laughter.

His eyes on her face, he leaned across the table to trail a single fingertip down her cheek and, his voice curiously husky, said, 'You should laugh more often; it suits you.'

Shaken to the core by that thistledown touch, she retorted sharply, 'I haven't had all that much to laugh about, lately…'

Hearing the bitterness in her own voice, Charlotte bit her

lip. Fool! she berated herself. Suppose he asked her why not?

But, cursing himself for his unthinking remark, Daniel said nothing.

Charlotte was fervently wishing that she had kept her feelings in check when the waiter arrived with leather-bound menus.

'Good evening, Mr Wolfe.'

'Evening, Georges.'

'If you have nothing special in mind, sir, may I suggest Chef's *Ficelle de Brantome*, followed by *Petits Rougets du Bassin au Cerfeuil*?'

'Yes, I've had them both before, and I must say they're excellent.'

Daniel looked enquiringly at his companion. 'Will stuffed savoury pancakes followed by baked red mullet with chervil suit you? Or would you prefer to choose for yourself?'

Charlotte, who had been struggling with her schoolgirl French, answered with relief, 'No, they'll be fine, thank you.'

When the waiter had moved away, as though unsure of her mood, her companion sat waiting quietly, his eyes on her face.

Seeing that he was leaving it to her to choose a topic of conversation, she began, 'You mentioned that Mr Shirland was related to you?'

'Yes, Richard is my aunt's son. Though that isn't why I employ him, so if you're thinking nepotism, forget it. He's well worth his salt.'

As though determined to be fair, Daniel added, 'Despite his somewhat ebullient manner, Richard is a brilliant businessman, and perhaps *because* of it he gets on well with people. Which makes him an asset on the social side. He's also popular with the staff.'

'That doesn't surprise me.'

'Do I gather you liked him?'

'Yes, I did. Very much.'

Seeing the flicker of vexation that crossed her companion's face she hugged herself before asking, 'Why did you tell him that I won't be starting work on Monday?'

'You're bound to feel shattered until you adjust to the time difference.'

'Surely by then I won't be likely to fall asleep at my desk?'

'Probably not, but I don't expect you to start work until after the holiday. These few days before Christmas can be used to get to know the city.'

'Are you this generous to all your employees?' she asked lightly.

Green eyes met grey. 'What would you like me to say? That you're special?'

She hesitated then said, 'Of course not. Why should I be special?'

'I can think of at least one reason.'

Her heart gave a little lurch, but all she said was, 'Oh?'

'This exchange scheme was my baby and I have a vested interest in the outcome. I'd like everything to work harmoniously, so I need to keep both participants happy.'

Brought down to earth with a bump, she queried, 'Then you'll be giving my London replacement the same amount of time off?'

Eyes glinting between thick dark lashes, he said, 'Matthew Curtis, the man who's taking your place, won't be going until after the holiday, so the answer's no.'

Deliberately, he added, 'I, on the other hand, *will* be taking that time off.'

His glance inviting the question, she was about to ask if there was any particular reason when their first course arrived, and she chickened out.

Finding herself unexpectedly hungry she tucked into the pancakes, enjoying their creamy filling of mushrooms, ham, and cheese.

Though Daniel had a healthy appetite she noticed that he ate neatly and precisely, neither hurrying nor dawdling.

'That was excellent,' she remarked when both their plates were empty.

'I'm pleased you liked it.' Then, with no change of tone, 'Go ahead and ask me.'

Deciding to play the innocent she queried, 'Ask you what?'

'Why I'm starting my Christmas holiday early.'

'OK,' she said flippantly, 'why *are* you starting your Christmas holiday early?'

'So I can show you around New York.'

Trying to hide her exhilaration she replied, 'That's extremely kind of you, but are you certain you can spare the time?'

'Quite certain. I'm looking forward to having a few days of leisure…'

He paused as, with well-drilled precision, their plates were removed, the main course served and their glasses refilled.

When the last waiter had retired, soft-footed, she pursued, 'So you're not the kind of businessman who's only happy when he's working?'

'Not at all. For the first few years after taking over my godfather's company I worked sixteen hours a day because I needed to.'

'And now?'

'I still work hard to consolidate what I have, so that when I marry I can relax and stand back a bit. I want to be able to play with my children, to take them places and teach them things, to spend time with my wife and family.'

This sketch of an ideal father didn't fit with his powerful

macho image, Charlotte thought dazedly, nor did it tie up with the portrait the papers had painted of him.

So which was the true picture? The decent, responsible family man? Or the playboy who could happily seduce a nineteen-year-old girl who was about to marry someone else?

Well, he was certainly the latter.

Was it possible he could be both? People's characters were rarely black and white, but varying shades of grey.

'What do you think of the mullet?' he asked.

Taken up with what he'd been saying she'd scarcely tasted it but she answered politely, 'It's very nice, thank you.'

Then, getting back to the nitty-gritty, 'In a magazine article I read you were described as an unrepentant bachelor.'

'But not a *confirmed* one. Until now I've been happy to keep things light but I'll soon be thirty and I'd like children while I'm still young enough to enjoy them...'

He sounded so sincere that little shivers of excitement began to run through her. If he was starting to think about a serious relationship there was at least a *chance* that her plan might succeed.

As casually as possible she asked, 'So if you're considering getting married how will you go about choosing a wife? I mean, what exactly will you be looking for?'

He gave her a thoughtful glance. 'As you seem to have kept up with the press's picture parade, what would your guess be?'

'Beauty as a prerequisite.'

'Wrong. For a relationship like marriage I'd put a degree of—suppose I use an out-moded word and say *purity* first.'

Seeing her surprise he said simply, 'I wouldn't want a wife who had slept around.'

'The old double standard,' she murmured.

'It isn't fair, I know, and I can't begin to defend myself. All the same, that's how I feel.'

She couldn't fault him for honesty.

'So beauty would come second?'

'Not even second. Kindness and intelligence are much more important. Beauty would be a bonus but not essential, so long as there was a strong physical attraction between us.'

'Then you plan to—'

He shook his head. 'No one can plan the chemistry between two people. It has to be spontaneous combustion.'

A little shiver running through her, she asked, 'What about money?'

'I have plenty.'

Recalling that most of the women he had escorted had been described as 'out of the top drawer', she suggested, 'Breeding?'

'I'll stick with character. Breeding can prove to be a two-edged sword.'

'What about love?'

He surprised her by answering firmly, 'If a marriage is to last a lifetime I would regard love as indispensable.'

'Love doesn't always guarantee that a relationship will work. Or at least *thinking* you're in love doesn't.'

'I take it you're speaking from experience?'

'Yes,' she admitted briefly.

'But you don't want to talk about it?'

'There's nothing much to talk about.'

Though Daniel was curious about her broken engagement, seeing her discomfort he refilled her glass and changed the subject.

'It would be the early hours of the morning in London. You must be feeling tired?'

'Just a bit,' she admitted.

'Well, we don't have to stay a minute longer than you want to.'

When the meal was over and coffee and liqueurs had been served and drunk, he rose and held out his hand. 'Shall we have one dance before we go?'

Shivering at the thought of being held in his arms, she hesitated. Then, reminding herself of her reason for being there, she made herself rise and put her hand into his.

As they moved on to the floor where the orchestra had begun to play an old classic, feeling her tautness he bent his head and said in her ear, 'Relax.'

He was a good dancer and, holding her in a light but firm clasp, he proved to be easy to follow.

After a while her tension melted away as ice gradually melted into the warmer water surrounding it.

Feeling her relax against him, he bent his head a little and, as the music suggested, placed his cheek against Charlotte's.

After the initial shock, against all expectations, Charlotte found herself enjoying the feel of his cheek against hers and the lingering scent of his aftershave.

When the dance was finished and the orchestra had changed to a slow foxtrot, he said, 'If you're ready to leave, just say the word.'

But, caught up in the mood and the music now, she no longer felt tired. 'I'm quite happy to stay,' she told him.

Loving the feel of her in his arms, he drew her close and, his cheek against hers once more, began to move to the smoochy music.

It was almost twelve-thirty and another bottle of champagne later before Daniel phoned the chauffeur to say they were ready to be picked up.

'Would you like one last glass of champagne while we wait?' he suggested.

Already feeling the effects of jet lag and too much to

drink, and knowing that she should say no, she found herself agreeing, 'Yes, please.'

When they finally got outside snow was falling gently, dressing the town in bridal white. Spellbound, she sighed, her head as light and floating as the feathery flakes.

Held securely in the crook of Daniel's arm, the journey home through the snowy streets passed like a hazy dream.

When they reached The Lilies she was vaguely aware of him thanking Perkins and wishing him goodnight before putting an arm around her waist and escorting her into a house that was warm and welcoming.

When, having tossed aside the overcoat he was carrying, he lifted her cloak from her shoulders, unsteady without his supporting arm she staggered a little.

Replacing his arm around her waist, he said, 'Straight up to bed, I think. You must be exhausted.'

'Not at all.' Throwing out an arm she sang, 'I could have danced all night,' and, feeling gay and insouciant, smiled at him.

'We almost did… But now it's time to sleep.'

Her head spinning gently, she was more than grateful for his support as they slowly climbed the stairs.

There wasn't a sound. But no doubt the housekeeper had already gone to bed…

Remembering fuzzily that Daniel had said *she* was occupying what used to be the housekeeper's suite, Charlotte found herself wondering where that good lady slept.

Trying not to slur her words, she queried, 'You mentioned that Perkins has a flat over the garages, but where does Mrs Morgan sleep?'

'When Kate first came to work for me she was a widow and it suited her to live in. But six months ago she remarried and now she only comes in on a daily basis during the week.'

Charlotte's insouciance disappeared like a gambler's

lucky streak. 'So she doesn't actually *live* here any longer?' Dimly she heard the dismay in her own voice.

'No, but she lives within easy walking distance, so it's no problem.'

It might not worry him but it did *her*, she thought through a haze of panic. Oh, why hadn't she asked that particular question earlier instead of relying on there being at least one other person in the house?

She recalled Carla saying seriously, 'Don't let the big bad Wolfe get you alone', and she hadn't intended to. But now here they were on their own. She was half-drunk and he was wholly dangerous.

And he wanted her… She was certain of that.

But all at once she was oddly convinced that, whatever happened, he wouldn't use force.

A man who could no doubt get almost any woman he wanted wouldn't need to… And, in any case, his ego probably wouldn't let him.

Her panic gave place to a kind of tipsy confidence. If she could just lead him on a little, make him all the keener…

As Carla had said on more than one occasion, 'If you want a man to run after you, run the other way'. So first she would give him a bit of encouragement, then she would run.

At her door she paused and, looking at him a shade owlishly, said, 'Thank you for a lovely evening.'

One hand beneath her elbow, he answered gravely, 'It was my pleasure.'

Lifting her face to his, like a flower to the sun, she mutely invited his kiss.

He wondered how her mouth would feel against his, how the curve of her breast would fit his hand, how she would feel beneath him…

But it was too soon.

Instead of accepting the invitation, he reached for the handle and opened her door.

What on earth was the matter with the man? she thought crossly. She had seen the lick of flame in his silvery eyes that told her he *wanted* to kiss her, but for some reason he was holding back.

Her inhibitions dispersed by the champagne bubbles, she slid her palms beneath the lapels of his jacket to steady herself while she stood on tiptoe to touch her lips to his.

Just for an instant his mouth stayed totally still and unresponsive. Then, as though the leash on his self-control had snapped, his arms went around her and he began to kiss her with a fierce passion that instantly aroused an answering hunger.

After a childhood of giving and receiving quiet, restrained affection she wasn't prepared for such a torrent of emotion and engulfed, swept away, all she could do was cling blindly to him while his mouth moved against hers.

How long he kissed her she never knew but, eyes closed and head reeling, her legs too weak to support her, she was incapable of any kind of protest by the time he lifted her in his arms and carried her into the bedroom.

When she stirred and opened her eyes it was to find a gleam of wintry sunshine slanting through the curtains and the pleasant room full of snowy light.

Still half asleep for a second or two, totally disorientated, she couldn't think where she was. Then her memory kicked in.

She was in New York... Staying at The Lilies with Daniel Wolfe...

Daniel Wolfe...

When they had got back last night he had kissed her, and then carried her into the bedroom.

Fully awake now, Charlotte sat bolt upright, her silky hair tumbling round her shoulders.

When her head stopped spinning two things became clear. She was alone in the big double bed and still wearing her underwear and silk stockings.

She took a deep, shuddering breath.

Yes, it was all coming back now. Though her eyes had been closed and her mind swimming in and out of consciousness she could hazily recall him laying her down on the bed before easing off her shoes, jacket and dress.

Then he had taken the pins from her chignon and, pulling up the duvet, tucked her hands beneath it before closing the door quietly behind him.

She had *him* to thank that nothing had happened. Not herself. *Certainly* not herself.

It was her attempt to lead him on that had sparked off the whole thing. She must have been mad! Thinking how it might have ended, she shuddered.

His kisses had affected her in a way that Peter's never had. If Daniel had turned on the heat she would have been unable to resist and surely he was too experienced not to have known that?

She frowned. If he *had* wanted her, as she'd thought, surely he would have taken advantage of the fact that she was in no state to say no?

But he hadn't taken advantage of her. He had put her to bed like a father putting a child to bed and walked away.

Why?

Had she only imagined he was interested? Although he had taken her out and announced his intention of showing her New York maybe he had thought of her as simply his employee and his guest?

If he had he must have been disgusted by her behaviour.

Looking at it from his point of view, she felt bitterly ashamed of the way she had acted, and recalling how he had kindly but firmly brushed off Maria she cringed mentally.

A wealthy man with his kind of charisma must be used to women throwing themselves at him and with no knowledge of what had driven her he had no doubt thought her cheap and silly.

And soon she would have to face him.

It wasn't a comfortable thought.

So where did that leave her campaign?

Probably nowhere on earth.

Vexed by her own stupidity, she glanced at her watch to find she had almost slept the clock round. It was time to get out of bed and face up to the mess she had made of things.

CHAPTER FIVE

SHOWERED and dressed in a fine woollen two-piece—the skirt plain, the top patterned in shades of grey and lavender—she began to brush her hair, the red-gold mass rippling beneath the strokes.

All at once she paused, recalling dimly how, after taking the pins from her chignon, Daniel had sat on the edge of the bed, stroking her hair and running his fingers through it.

The memory was oddly poignant and when she twisted the shining strands into a coil and anchored it with a crocodile clip her hands were unsteady.

Unable to account for that poignancy she sighed and, feeling confused and vulnerable, reluctantly made her way downstairs.

Though a log fire crackled cheerfully in the grate and a discarded newspaper lay on the settee the living-room was empty.

A tap on the study door eliciting no response, she went through to the kitchen to find him standing by the sink.

Shirt sleeves rolled up to expose muscular forearms, a tea towel tucked into the belt of his stone-coloured trousers, he was feeding quartered oranges into a juicer.

His dark hair was a little rumpled and, in spite of the unexpected domesticity, he looked devastatingly masculine and attractive.

Glancing up, he said, 'Good morning... Or, more accurately, good afternoon.'

His look held nothing of the contempt or condemnation she had half-expected.

'Your timing's excellent,' he remarked cheerfully. 'I've just started to prepare lunch.'

The last thing she had expected was such casual friendliness and she simply stood and stared at him.

'I hope you slept well?'

She swallowed. 'Very well.'

'No hangover, I trust?' He smiled at her.

His mouth and teeth were excellent, and the sheer charm of that smile made her pulses race and left her weak at the knees.

'No, I feel fine, thank you,' she managed, and was aware that her voice sounded husky and impeded.

He filled a couple of glasses with juice and handed her one. 'I hope you like omelette *aux fines herbes*? If you don't, I can manage garlic prawns or—'

'I'm sorry about last night,' she said in a rush. 'A combination of jet lag and too much to drink no doubt played a part, but it still doesn't excuse my behaviour.'

He shook his head. 'I'm the one who should be apologizing. I ought to have realized that when you were so tired champagne wasn't a good idea. It's a miracle you stayed on your feet as long as you did.

'Now then, what's it to be?'

For a moment his easy dismissal of the whole thing threw her. Then, pulling herself together, she said, 'An omelette would be lovely.'

'I'm not so sure about *lovely*… Edible, I hope, but you may find my cooking leaves a lot to be desired.'

'I'm surprised you don't—' She broke off abruptly.

'Pay someone else to do it?'

'Yes,' she admitted.

'Apart from the fact that I've got to rather like having the house to myself at the weekends, I quite enjoy practising my culinary skills.'

Grinning evilly at her, he added, 'And now I've got a captive guest, so to speak, to try them out on.'

Responding to that wicked glee, she crossed her eyes and, clutching dramatically at her throat, made a gurgling sound.

He burst out laughing.

Straightening her face, she queried, 'Have you a cellar here?'

'Why do you ask?'

'You seem remarkably unconcerned about poisoning your guests.'

Looking highly amused he murmured, 'Shades of arsenic? Don't worry. I promise I'll try everything first.'

His teeth gleaming, his grey eyes alight with laughter, he was almost irresistible and she felt hollow inside.

Aware that she was in grave danger of liking him, she sighed. If only the past could be wiped away, like chalk from a blackboard. But of course that was impossible. What was past couldn't be altered.

Nor could the fact that, no matter how wholesome and attractive Daniel Wolfe might appear at this moment, he had a darker, much less pleasant, side.

Noting her change of expression, he said ironically, 'If it's going to seriously worry you we could always go out for lunch.'

Drumming up a smile, she shook her head decidedly. 'I wouldn't dream of it. Now you've whetted my appetite I can't wait to try your cooking.'

'There speaks a woman who's brave... Or should I say foolhardy?'

'I'm sure you make wonderful omelettes.'

'Well, the proof of the pudding, and all that...'

The table was already set and, pulling out a chair, he added, 'Better sit down and say your prayers.'

Charlotte sat and sipped her orange juice while she

watched in fascination as he beat the eggs and made a large, fluffy omelette.

Peter would never set foot in a kitchen if he could help it saying, with barely hidden contempt, that it was a woman's domain.

But, all his movements quick and deft, Daniel appeared to be as at home working in a kitchen as in an office, without it detracting one iota from his powerful masculinity.

Folding the golden circle neatly in half, he cut it across and slid each piece on to a warm plate, before taking a seat opposite.

The simple meal, accompanied by crusty bread and a crisp green salad was delicious and she said so.

'Lavish praise indeed,' he murmured. 'Just for that I'll take you sightseeing this afternoon. Where would you like to start?'

'I'd love a walk through Central Park.'

'I take it you have some boots and really warm clothing with you?'

'Yes.'

'Then Central Park it is.'

Over the next few days, though the snowy weather continued, they went out from morning till night, seeing and doing everything there was to see and do, sometimes by car, quite often on foot.

Amongst other things, they visited Battery Park, saw the Statue of Liberty, went to the Empire State building, had breakfast at Tiffany's and dinner at the Rainbow Room.

As well as following what Daniel called 'the tourist trail' he showed her the lesser known parts of Manhattan where there was a real community spirit and where, almost on the same block, poverty and riches rubbed shoulders.

From street vendors they bought wonderful-smelling brazier-roasted corn cobs and hot chestnuts, laughing as they burnt their fingers on the shells. And on their way to see the Winter Garden they stopped for coffee at a West Side Mission for the Homeless that, she learnt from the priest, Daniel had set up and supported almost single-handed.

He took her to eat in Chinatown and Little Italy and in small basement restaurants where the tablecloths were checked gingham, candles burnt in empty wine bottles and the food was good.

When, growing uncomfortable about the amount of money he was spending on her, she ventured to protest, he said drily, 'If it's worrying you I'll take steps to have it deducted from your salary.'

'But I haven't officially started yet,' she pointed out carefully.

'You should have been getting paid from the day you arrived over here, so when you actually *start* doesn't come into it. No one will argue about that.'

'If you say so. You're the boss.'

Grinning, he told her, 'It has its compensations.'

One afternoon, after watching skaters on the Pond, Daniel arranged for them to have a horse and carriage ride through frosty Central Park, and in the evening they went to a concert of George Gershwin's music.

She started to recognize some of the special sights and sounds and smells that made up New York, and gain a real insight into what made it tick.

But, as well as learning a lot about New York, she learnt a lot about the man himself.

He proved to be sanguine and even-tempered, with wide-ranging interests and a *joie de vivre* that was infectious. Knowledgeable and articulate, he was happy to both talk and listen, but he was also a man who was quite comfortable with silence.

She discovered that he had a dry sense of humour and a

strong sense of justice and, though women almost invariably turned to give him a second look, he seemed to have no personal vanity.

Over and above everything she was conscious of the chemistry between them, the pull of his attraction. Whatever they were doing she was *aware* of him, always on a fine edge. When in his company her senses seemed better tuned and focused; sounds were clearer, colours brighter, scents more evocative.

For his part—though from time to time she glimpsed a look in his eyes that made her heart stand still—he treated her with a careful camaraderie.

Yet there was a great deal more to it than mere friendliness. It was almost as if he was quietly courting her, she thought, and smiled, amused by the old-fashioned word.

But though in public he sometimes took her hand and occasionally put an arm around her, when they were alone he never attempted to either touch her or kiss her. Each evening he accompanied her upstairs and said a chaste goodnight outside her door.

Taught a lesson by the last fiasco, and well satisfied with the way things were going, she took care not to drink too much and resisted any temptation to play with fire.

If he hadn't been who he was it would have been one of the happiest times of her life. She had discovered a lot to like about him and nothing to dislike. Except his past record.

When Christmas Eve was only a couple of days away they had an early dinner in the Village Tavern before going to an open-air carol concert in Washington Square Park.

It was a bitterly cold night and, rather than fetch Perkins out, Daniel hailed a cab to take them back to The Lilies.

When they reached home, still chilled to the bone, it was to find a single standard lamp burning and the lights on the Christmas tree sparkling with festive cheer.

Mrs Morgan had thoughtfully stoked up the fire before she left and the welcome aroma of coffee keeping hot drifted in from the kitchen.

After disposing of their outdoor things, Daniel stirred the piled-up embers into life and, having added a couple of fresh logs, suggested to Charlotte, 'Why don't you sit in front of the fire while I get the coffee?'

Only too pleased to obey, she took a seat on the couch and stretched her cold feet towards the blaze.

'They'll never get warm that way.'

Crouching in front of her, he slipped off her boots and, taking first one then the other of her slim feet between his palms, began to rub some life back into them.

Since her mother died Charlotte had always been the one to tend and cherish, and the caring gesture made her breath catch in her throat as she sat still and silent, looking down at his dark head.

'Better?' he asked after a little while.

'Much better, thank you,' she answered huskily and, overwhelmingly conscious of his nearness, his touch, breathed a sigh of relief when he rose to his feet and moved away.

Making an effort to calm herself, she sat staring at the leaping flames and the way the shadows flickered on the walls and ceiling. But she could still feel the touch of his hands and see how his thick dark hair, though cut fairly short, attempted to curl into his nape.

She had wanted to touch that hair, to hold his head against her breast.

No! She mustn't think that. She must keep reminding herself what kind of man he really was. He might *seem* to be different, but he wasn't really. A leopard didn't change its spots...

The kitchen door opened and he was back.

'Here we are,' he said cheerfully and, handing her a mug,

added, 'I thought the occasion called for a spot of brandy to really warm us up.'

Taking a seat beside her, he stretched his long legs towards the flames.

As the soft cushions gave beneath him his muscular thigh brushed hers and she jumped convulsively, almost spilling her coffee.

Instantly, he moved away a little, giving her space, but the air was suddenly thick with a sexual tension Charlotte wasn't sure she could handle.

Daniel was staring straight ahead and a quick glance at his handsome profile showed that his mouth was firm and his jaw set, as though he was exercising great self-control.

Desperate to defuse the situation, and needing something to say until her coffee mug was empty and she could escape to her own suite, she sought for a topic of conversation.

Though more than a week had passed nothing had been said about moving into the company apartment and, happy with things as they were, Charlotte hadn't broached the subject.

But, purely for the look of the thing, she couldn't go on leaving it.

Making up her mind, she jumped in with both feet. 'I imagine the company apartment must be free by now, so I was wondering when you'd like me to move in?'

There was a barely perceptible pause before he answered evenly, 'Well, not just yet. When I had it checked out the other day it wasn't as pristine as it should have been, and I've given orders for it to be redecorated first...'

Though the conversation was a little forced, a shade stilted, at least they were talking.

The moment of danger seemed to be passed.

'The workmen are due to move in tomorrow,' he went on, 'and the job won't be completed until after the holiday.

So I'm afraid you're stuck with me for the time being. That
is, if you don't mind?'

A little flustered, she asked, 'But aren't you going away
for Christmas?'

'I'd considered going Upstate to the family lodge for a
few days. If I do—'

'I can move into a hotel as soon as you like,' she offered
hastily.

'And be on your own over the holiday? I wouldn't hear
of it. As I was about to say, I'd like you to go with me.'

She shook her head. 'There's no way I can foist myself
on to your parents at Christmas time. Whatever would they
think?'

'Had they been alive I'm sure they would have been
delighted, but they were killed in an accident on the
Interstate while I was still at college.'

'I'm sorry,' she said quietly.

'Apart from Richard and his parents, I've no close family
left in New York State.'

'You've no brothers or sisters?'

'One younger sister. Glenda married a Canadian and
lives in Vancouver... So you see, if it wasn't for you I'd
be spending Christmas on my own.'

Then coaxingly, 'Wouldn't you like to see the Catskill
Mountains?'

'Very much, but—' About to make an excuse, she hesitated. What was the point of staying alone in a hotel? She
must make the most of this chance to be with him.

But she could be playing with fire. Suppose they were
alone in the middle of nowhere? Whether he simply *wanted*
her or was starting to get serious he was a practised seducer...

She'd better be sure she wanted to play this game.

Though if he *was* interested wouldn't he have tried to

seduce her before now, rather than holding back as he had done…?

'Maybe you've had enough of my company?' he hazarded when she remained silent.

'No, it isn't that,' she denied, replacing her mug.

'So what is it?'

'Well, I—'

'Perhaps you don't like the idea of spending the holiday quietly? If that's the reason we could always stay in New York.'

'I like New York… In fact, you could say it was love at first sight… But it would be nice to spend Christmas in the Catskills.'

She sensed his pleasure and relief as he said, 'Then it's all settled. I'll talk to Mrs Munroe, who takes care of the place for me, and we'll travel up on Christmas Eve.'

So they wouldn't be alone after all.

'Sounds marvellous,' she admitted, rising to her feet. 'I've wanted to see the Catskills ever since I read *Rip van Winkle* at school.'

As he stood up to join her she added, 'But I suppose the whole area must have changed considerably since then?'

'Not as much as you might imagine. Though in parts a lot of the hemlock has disappeared from the slopes, there are still plenty around the lodge.'

'Handy for poisoning off unwanted neighbours,' she remarked lightly.

Laughing, he told her, 'I meant the hemlock fir or spruce, rather than the plant. The foliage of the trees smells like hemlock when it's crushed…'

Suddenly, with no idea how it had happened, Charlotte found they were gazing into each other's eyes. An instant later she saw the amusement die out of his, to be replaced by a look that shook her to her very soul.

In response to that look a chasm seemed to open at her feet and unconsciously she swayed towards him.

His arms went around her and then he was kissing her, his mouth warm and urgent.

Suddenly there was nothing in the whole wide world but this man—no past, no future, only the present and the feelings that drove her.

As she clung to him she was dimly aware of him taking the pins from her hair... Running his fingers through the tumbled mass... Holding her head between his palms as he continued to kiss her.

When his lips wandered away to explore the soft skin beneath her chin and the warm column of her throat she shivered with delight.

Then, one hand spread across her spine, he used the other to trace the slender curves of breast and waist and hip. Even through the fine wool of her two-piece his touch was electrifying, and every nerve in her body sang into life.

She felt such an overpowering ache for him that she couldn't breathe, and when he began to unbutton her top she would willingly have helped him, had he needed any help.

But with an assured deftness he was already slipping it off her shoulders and freeing her arms. A moment later her skirt was tossed aside, her underslip quickly disposed of, and he was unclipping her bra.

She could hear her own heart thundering as he ran his hands over her naked breasts, cupping their soft weight lightly, delicately.

When his thumbs brushed over the dusky-pink nipples she gasped and shuddered convulsively and, her legs so weak they would no longer support her, sank down on the sheepskin rug.

Pulling a cushion from the settee, he settled her head

tenderly on it and, without taking his eyes off her, began to swiftly discard his own clothing.

She was long-legged and slender with curving hips and small perfectly-shaped breasts. Firelight gilded her flawless skin and turned her glorious hair to fiery gold.

Hardly daring to breathe, he stood for a second or two gazing down at her, thinking he had never seen anything so lovely.

Then, smiling into lambent green eyes that looked dazed with passion, he stretched out beside her, murmuring, 'My beautiful darling.'

Despite the urgency he felt, a lover of subtlety and finesse, he caressed her face and neck and shoulders, her ribcage and slim waist, with a thistledown touch, before sliding a hand down her flat stomach to explore the nest of silky hair and the smooth skin of her inner thighs.

Bending to nuzzle his face against her breasts, eyes closed, heavy dark lashes lying on his cheeks, he searched blindly for a nipple and licked it into firmness before his mouth, warm and moist, closed around it.

As he suckled contentedly she began to make soft sounds in her throat, little wordless pleas and, on fire for him, moved her hips in a reflex action as old as time.

In response to that tacit urging she felt the muscular warmth of his lithe body cover hers, and with his first strong thrust there was nothing but spiralling sensation until her whole being was flooded with ecstasy.

As it slowly ebbed she became aware of the weight of his dark head on her breast and the heat of the fire on her bare limbs.

At the same moment he stirred and raised his head to kiss her mouth—a long, slow kiss full of sweetness and passion.

Then he was easing himself away and, unwilling to let

him go, with an unintelligible murmur she put her arms round his neck.

'That's right,' he said encouragingly and, gathering her up in his arms added, 'I could stay here all night but in a while it'll start to get cold, so bed's the best place.'

His bedroom was full of bright moonlight and in a moment her head was on soft pillows and she was covered by a warm duvet.

He slid in beside her and, drawing her close, simply held her, savouring his triumph. Not only was she his at last, but he was experienced enough to know how totally inexperienced she was and, fiercely glad, he gave thanks.

After a while, desire stirring again, he began to kiss her once more. The first urgency over, his lovemaking was even sweeter as, slowly and leisurely with hands and mouth and tongue, he set out to pleasure her, finding his own satisfaction in her little gasps and moans and shudders of delight.

Several times, she whispered, 'Please... Oh, please...'

But, refusing to be hurried, with rare skill and judgement he kept her hovering on the brink.

Just when she thought she couldn't stand another minute of such exquisite torture, she felt his welcome weight once more, and buried her face against his throat as they moved together.

This time the rapture, though just as explosive, was somehow deeper, even more earth-shaking, and afterwards, her head pillowed on his shoulder, they lay utterly content while their heart-rate and breathing returned to something like normal.

Daniel was about to speak to her when, glancing down, he saw that she was deeply asleep, her oval face a little flushed.

Studying the straight nose and high cheekbones, the curved brows and long curly lashes that were darker than her hair, the mouth that in sleep looked innocent and vulnerable, he had to resist a powerful urge to kiss her, to have her wake and smile at him.

Finding he was on too much of a high to sleep, he lay for a long time cradling her close, listening to her soft breathing and enjoying the feel of her naked body against his.

When Charlotte stirred and opened her eyes it was still very early, though the snow was making the strange room light. For a few seconds, disorientated, she wondered where she was. Then, like a thunderclap, came instant and complete remembrance.

Last night Daniel Wolfe had made love to her. Even now he was lying beside her in his bed.

No, that couldn't be so. It couldn't! Unable to breathe, feeling as though she'd been kicked in the solar plexus, she tried desperately to reject what she knew only too well to be true.

Giving up the impossible task, she flayed herself. How *could* she have let such a thing happen? How *could* she have slept with the man who was responsible for her brother's death?

But she had. Willingly. Eagerly.

She couldn't even salvage her pride by telling herself he'd seduced her; she had as good as thrown herself at him.

When Peter, a man she had thought she loved, had been at his most pressing she had easily resisted his pleas and arguments, so what had made her give herself to a man she hated?

Or did she?

She *ought* to hate him, and part of her still did, but suddenly, hopelessly, she knew it wasn't so simple.

From the beginning, though she had never really admitted it, she had wanted him physically. But her feelings were a great deal more tangled and complicated than merely *wanting* him.

Last night their coming together had been so right, so intense, it was almost impossible to believe that lust had been the only driving force. Some much deeper emotion must have existed.

But Daniel wasn't into emotion. When she had asked him, he had admitted that he was used to having sex on a safe, no-strings-involved, purely recreational basis.

Her mind becoming suddenly cool and lucid, she saw clearly that if any deeper emotion *had* existed it had been solely on *her* side.

Carefully turning her head, she looked at the man stretched out beside her. Just the sight of him made her heart lurch.

He was lying on his back breathing quietly and steadily, one hand flung towards her, as though even in sleep he had been unwilling to let her go.

The duvet had slipped down, and the smooth olive skin of his throat and muscular shoulders glowed clear and healthy. His dark hair was rumpled and his long lashes spread like fans on his hard cheekbones.

With morning stubble adorning his jaw and his firm mouth relaxed in sleep he looked so attractive and virile that she felt her pulses leap in response to his sheer maleness.

For a moment she had to fight down a mad desire to waken him, to see those grey eyes open, to have him smile at her with a promise of delight as he reached out to draw her close…

Her stomach clenched and she closed her eyes tightly, as if to shut out temptation.

But if, in the cold light of day, she was still tempted by a man she had so much cause to hate, what chance had she got of resisting him in the future?

Though it wasn't only sex. She could have loved this man…

Did love this man. The realization came simply in the end.

For a while she sat as though turned to stone, stunned by the ambivalence of her own feelings.

But hadn't someone once said that love and hatred, two of the most powerful of all human emotions, were opposite sides of the same coin?

Well, somewhere along the line the coin had been flipped. While she had been trying to make him fall in love with her she had somehow, despite the anger and hatred she'd felt, fallen in love with him.

But how had it happened?

As Carla had said, *pride builds a lonely house.* However had Daniel Wolfe managed to get inside so quickly?

Though this was no sudden thing. It hadn't just happened overnight. From the start she had been drawn to pictures of him, fascinated against her will. He had disturbed her deeply, made her uncomfortable by his sheer maleness.

While refusing to face up to the reason, she had known he was dangerous. That was why, at first, she had avoided him so assiduously.

But was it possible to fall in love with a picture?

That in turn posed the question, how *did* one fall in love?

Surely sight was the first of the senses to be involved. What someone looked like was the beginning of the process. Only then did one go on to ask, Is he appealing? Does he attract in other ways?

Daniel had attracted her, big time.

From the start the chemistry between them had been powerful but, intent on her scheme for revenge, she had done her best to ignore it.

At some level she had been aware that she was in danger, but she hadn't thought for an instant that it was possible to care for the man who had caused her so much distress and heartache.

How could she have known that he would get under her skin? Make her love him? Capture her heart, even while she was trying to capture his?

Yet he had. And such a love was hopeless.

If you juggle with knives you're likely to get cut, had been one of her father's sayings.

Foolishly, she had juggled with knives, and now she was bleeding. All she could do was lick her wounds and go.

Though how could she bear to leave him?

If she didn't, the voice of reason warned, she would become his plaything and end up losing her pride and self-respect.

Perhaps she could just stay until Christmas was over—she found herself trying to bargain with common sense—if she took care to keep things on a platonic footing...

But in her heart of hearts she knew she couldn't. Her feelings for him made her much too vulnerable. The only possible thing she could do was go, and go quickly. Make sure she never saw Daniel Wolfe again.

At least that way she would regain some small vestige of pride and self-respect.

But just the thought of leaving him made her feel as though a giant fist had closed around her heart and was squeezing the life out of it.

Sucking in air, she faced the fact that if she couldn't find the strength to leave now it would get more and more difficult, until it became impossible.

Then, sooner or later, *he* would walk away from *her* and she would have nothing left, not even her pride.

Softly and with infinite care, knowing that if he awoke and smiled at her she would be lost, she eased herself out of bed.

Her bare feet on the dark oak floorboards made whispers

of sound and she held her breath as she crept to the door. To her relief, the ornate iron handle moved easily under her hand and, without daring to look back, she slipped through the door and closed it gently behind her.

A few seconds later she reached her own suite of rooms safely.

Refusing to think, just blindly obeying the need to run, she showered and dressed with all speed. Scared to death that if he awoke early and came looking for her, her resolve might weaken, she collected her belongings as fast as possible and bundled them into her case anyhow.

Then, in her stocking feet, she tiptoed along the landing and down the stairs to the living-room where the Christmas tree lights sparkled and a single standard lamp still glowed.

The grate was full of half-burnt logs and whitish ash and the mugs they had used the previous night stood on the coffee table. Scattered on the settee lay their discarded clothing.

A hollow, wrenching feeling inside her, she pulled on her boots and grabbed her coat and, hurrying to the door, let herself out into a street that was just stirring into life.

CHAPTER SIX

THE air was bitter and overhead the sky gleamed pearly-grey like the inside of a mussel shell. There had been more snow overnight and a pristine white carpet covered the steps and pavement.

It was crisp underfoot and, the heavy case banging against her leg, she walked away, only half aware of the tears that poured down her cheeks in a steady, silent stream.

Swopping the case from one hand to the other, she had reached the end of Carver Street and turned into one of the busier thoroughfares before it occurred to her that she hadn't the faintest idea where she was going, or what she intended to do.

Her only thought to get away, she hadn't stopped to make plans.

But now she must.

As luck would have it, Benny's Breakfast Bar was just across the street and thankfully it was open.

Putting down her case, she fished in her bag for a handkerchief, blew her nose and dried her face. Then, having waited at the lights for a 'walk' signal, she crossed and went inside.

Benny's was warm and steamy, with vinyl-topped tables and red plastic chairs. At the bar a big man wearing only jeans and a sleeveless vest was tucking into a pile of greasy-looking doughnuts, while several others were eating their way through plates of eggs and hash browns.

She was the only woman in there and, choosing a cramped table for one in the far corner, Charlotte left her case by the wall and went to the bar to order coffee.

Looking at her curiously, the plump-faced, balding man with *Benny* emblazoned in red on his white tee shirt, asked, 'Doughnuts?'

Her stomach churning and disliking doughnuts at the best of times she answered, 'No thanks.'

Returning to her table with the coffee, which proved to be good and hot and strong, she wondered if Daniel was awake yet, and if he'd missed her...

Just thinking about him brought such a stab of pain that she sat quite still, breathing as though her lungs were full of shards of glass.

When the pain eased a little, making a determined effort to put him right out of her mind, she tried to concentrate on what to do for the best.

Paying for the coffee had made her realize how very little money she had, barely enough to pay her bus fare to JFK.

But what was the use of going to the airport when she had no money for a ticket?

Sighing, she faced the fact that the need to act so precipitately had left her in a real mess.

Oh, why hadn't she considered the possibility of such a contingency arising before she had agreed to fly to the States?

The answer was stark and uncompromising. Even if she *had* she'd been so obsessed with her plan for revenge that she would still have taken the chance.

Sighing, she admitted that she had behaved like an absolute idiot from start to finish.

For the first time she wished she had taken out a credit card. But having to contend with Tim's college fees, and keep him in clothes and pocket money, she had been wary of running up debts she might not be able to pay.

So now what was she to do?

For a while she explored every avenue she could think of, without success. Then, like a gleam of light in the darkness, she realized that Carla would help. Of course she would.

Some of her immediate anxiety faded.

Carla should be able to book a return flight to London on *her* credit card.

If there was a seat available so close to Christmas.

But surely there would be *one*?

Clinging to that hope, she made her way over to the public phone and, having checked that she had plenty of change for the call, dialled the operator and asked to be put through to the Bayswater flat.

A few seconds later she heard it ringing out.

It kept ringing.

'There seems to be no answer, caller,' a voice informed her.

Of course, she'd forgotten the time difference! Carla would be at work...

'I'd like you to try another number,' Charlotte said quickly, and gave her the phone number of the boutique.

'Still no answer, caller.' The operator sounded more than a little impatient.

'Please keep it ringing,' Charlotte begged. 'There's bound to be someone there.'

After quite a lengthy wait a harassed-sounding Macy answered.

Charlotte identified herself quickly and asked, 'Can I speak to Carla?'

'She's not here.'

'When will she be back?'

'Not until after Christmas. She's on her way to Scotland.'

Of course. With so much happening she'd totally forgotten. Clutching at straws now, Charlotte asked, 'Can you tell me exactly *where* in Scotland?'

'Andrew's parents live in Dundee, I believe.'

'Have you either the address or the phone number?'

''Fraid not.'

'Any idea when Carla will be back?'

'The twenty-seventh. Look, I must go. I'm on my own and there's a shop full.'

A second later the receiver was replaced.

With a feeling akin to despair, Charlotte went back to her table and sat down again.

'More coffee?' A glass jug in his hand, Benny was standing by her elbow.

About to say please, she remembered how few dollars she had left and started to shake her head.

His eyes on her pale face he said, 'Go ahead, lady. You look as if you could use it, and it's on the house.'

'Thanks.'

Grateful for his kindness, she accepted the refill and sipped while she worried over her problem. A problem which, with hardly any money, nowhere to go, and Christmas only two days away, had begun to assume terrifying proportions.

It would be ironic if she ended up spending Christmas in the West Side Mission for the Homeless, she thought grimly, and with no one else to turn to she might well.

Then, with a sudden flare of hope, she realized that maybe there *was* someone else. Richard Shirland. He'd said, 'If you do find you need help of any kind…just let me know.'

The snag was, he was Daniel's cousin.

All the same he seemed to be his own man. Though he must have realized that Daniel wasn't happy about his interest in their new employee he hadn't let it deter him.

As she hesitated, worried about asking for help from someone so close to Daniel, a voice asked, 'You all finished?'

Startled, she looked up to find a dark, burly man looming

over her. He had a plate of breakfast in one hand and some cutlery in the other.

'Yes… Sorry.'

Whilst she'd been thinking the small bar had filled up. Guiltily, she vacated the chair and, settling the strap of her bag over her shoulder, picked up her case and made her way to the door.

The case felt as though it weighed a ton and, after sitting so long in the steamy heat of the café, the outside air struck even colder.

Shivering, she began to walk. But it was no use just walking aimlessly, she told herself sternly. She had to do *something*, and Richard Shirland seemed to be her only hope, so it was a chance she would have to take. He seemed to be a decent sort, and if she begged him not to say a word to Daniel…

But it was quite a way Uptown and there was a limit to how far she could walk carrying her case.

Could she afford a taxi?

A quick mental check of how many dollars she had left reassured her that she could. *Just.*

As she walked, she scanned the road. Luck was with her and in less than a minute she had spotted an empty yellow cab cruising by and hailed it.

Heaving her case in, she climbed in after it and said breathlessly, 'The Lloyd Wolfe Building on Central Park East, please.'

Then, her legs all of a tremble, she sat down abruptly. For better or for worse, she was committed.

When the cab dropped Charlotte outside the prestigious glass and concrete Lloyd Wolfe Building she made her way through heavy, smoked-glass doors and into an imposing marble-floored lobby.

The reception area was sleek and modern, with chrome and glass tables, and blue suede furniture.

'Can I help you?' the smart young brunette behind the desk asked.

'Could I speak to Mr Richard Shirland, please?' Catching sight of a large clock which showed it was still only twenty past eight, she added, 'That is, if he's in?'

'If you'd care to give me your name, I'll check with his secretary.'

'My name's Charlotte Michaels.'

'Perhaps you'd like to take a seat for a moment, Miss Michaels?'

'Thank you.' Charlotte sat down in one of the suede chairs grouped nearby, her case by her side.

She heard the receptionist say, 'Mrs Cope, there's a Miss Michaels would like to speak to Mr Shirland.'

During the pause that followed Charlotte found herself wondering what on earth she would do if Richard Shirland wasn't coming in? If he'd started his Christmas holiday early?

She was trying to push the uncomfortable prospect away when the receptionist replaced the phone and said, 'Mr Shirland will be down in just a moment, Miss Michaels.'

'Thank you.'

She was still smiling her relief when a petite young blonde came in through the main entrance and, head-down, started to cross the lobby. There was something so familiar about her that Charlotte found herself staring at the newcomer as though mesmerized.

As she drew level the girl glanced up and their eyes met. Feeling as though she had walked into an invisible plate glass window, she recognized the blonde as Tim's ex-fiancée, Janice.

Looking equally startled, for an instant the blonde's step faltered then, her gaze fixed straight ahead, she hurried on.

When Charlotte had resumed work after Tim's death it was to find that, without a word, Janice had given in her notice and left both her job and the small flat where she and Tim had been so happy.

But what on earth was the girl doing here?

Janice reached the elevator just as the doors slid open and Richard Shirland appeared. They said good morning to each other as they passed.

Spotting Charlotte, Richard came hurrying over. 'Miss Michaels, how nice to see you again.' His pleasant face beaming, he took her hand, adding, 'You're an early bird.'

'I wondered if you'd be here,' she told him abstractedly.

'As I needed some facts and figures for this morning's finance meeting I came in about six-thirty. I can get a lot more done while it's quiet.'

'The blonde girl you've just spoken to,' Charlotte said. 'I thought I recognized her.'

'You may well have done. Before she started working in our General Office Miss Jeffries was employed at our London headquarters. I gather Daniel had her transferred to New York.'

Charlotte clenched her teeth. Not content with seducing the girl, Daniel had brought her over here so their affair could continue...

Which meant that when she'd asked him if he had a current lady friend he'd been lying when he had said no. He'd also lied about sticking to one woman at a time.

Feeling as though a noose of barbed wire was slowly tightening around her heart, she knew she'd been right to leave him and run.

Suddenly noticing her case Richard asked, 'You've left The Lilies?'

'Yes.'

He frowned. 'I'm afraid the apartment isn't habitable. Daniel said you wouldn't be moving in until after Christmas and the place is full of ladders and workmen.'

'He did mention that it was being redecorated, but I...'

She hesitated, biting her lip to hold back a sudden, treacherous surge of emotion.

'Something wrong?' Richard asked.

'Yes, I'm afraid so,' she admitted in a rush. 'I badly need your help.'

'Anything I can do…? Is the problem to do with your job?'

She shook her head. 'It's a personal matter.' In spite of all her efforts her eyes filled with tears.

Glancing around the foyer, which was starting to resemble Times Square with staff arriving for work, he said, 'We can't stay here, and in a little while my office will be like a beehive… Have you had breakfast yet?'

'No.'

'Great! Neither have I. Look, give me a minute to have a word with my secretary, and then we'll go and have a bite to eat while we talk.'

He was back quite quickly and, having stashed her case behind the reception desk, he led her a short distance along the block to Masons, a quiet little coffee bar.

Pleasantly warm, with an attractive decor, it was as far removed from Benny's as it was possible to be.

Choosing a booth in the far corner, he ordered ham and cheese bagels and coffee and, with rare sensitivity, said nothing until they arrived.

Then he suggested quietly, 'It's to do with Daniel, I suppose?'

Wondering just how much to tell him, she hesitated before saying, 'For reasons I'd rather not go into, I felt forced to leave The Lilies.'

'What did he do, make a heavy pass at you? No, forget it, I shouldn't have asked. Just tell me what you're planning to do.'

'Go home.'

'Back to England?' He sounded stunned.

'Yes.'

'That bad, is it?'

Seeing the anger in his blue eyes, she assured him quickly, 'It's not what you think. Honestly. Though I do want to leave New York as soon as possible.'

'I'm afraid there just aren't any available seats this close to Christmas. I know someone who's checked out every single flight without success.'

'I was afraid that might be the case,' she said.

'So how can I help you?'

'Until my London flatmate gets back from her Christmas holiday, and can book a return flight for me, I need somewhere to stay.'

'Well, there are plenty of hotels in New York.'

'I don't have a credit card and I've no money,' she said flatly.

Looking amazed he said, 'Well, why didn't you ask Daniel for a loan?'

'I *couldn't* ask Daniel.'

'He may have his faults but I can't see him—'

'I left this morning before he was awake.' Then, realizing how very revealing her words were, she blushed furiously.

Richard's fair brows drew together in a frown. 'You mean he doesn't know you're gone?'

'I dare say he will by now.' She wondered if he would be angry.

'Well, if you don't want to deal with Daniel direct the company will advance you any amount you need, and when you start work again after Christmas—'

'I won't be starting work again… At least, not for Wolfe International.'

'Then I'll make it a personal loan,' he offered.

Charlotte, after struggling for so many years to support Tim, had a horror of being in debt. Only too aware that when she *did* get home she would have no job and she would owe Carla for her air ticket she said, 'Thank you. That's very kind of you.'

Then carefully, 'But, while I may be forced to borrow a little, I simply can't afford to stay in a hotel… Surely there must be a cheaper option?'

'Apart from youth hostels and one or two student centres, cheap accommodation isn't easy to find in New York. I understand that there are some private homes who do Bed and Breakfast, but I don't hold out much hope of getting one at this time of the year.'

Hearing her despairing sigh he said, 'If necessary, I could clear the decorators out of the company apartment.'

'I couldn't stay there.' If Daniel did by any chance look for her…

'You could always come home with me.'

As she started to shake her head he said quickly, 'It's all very proper. I'm living with the family at present while my apartment block is being renovated. Unfortunately, I'm due to fly down to Florida straight after this morning's meeting, but I'm sure my parents would be only too pleased to—'

'Thank you, but I wouldn't want to involve either you or your parents to that extent…'

'Got it!' he exclaimed jubilantly as her words tailed off. 'It won't be what you're used to… In fact, it's pretty grim, I gather… But you would have a roof over your head and a clean bed to sleep in.'

'That's all I need.'

'Sure?'

'Quite sure.'

'Then stay here and finish your breakfast while I have a quick word with Martin and see if I can fix things.'

In just over ten minutes he was back. 'If you're ready to go?'

She picked up her bag and rose to her feet.

Hurrying her to the door, he added apologetically, 'Sorry

about all the rush, but my car's illegally parked and I've already had one ticket this month.'

Opening the door of a blue saloon parked half on the sidewalk he said, 'Jump in and as soon as we get moving I'll tell you what all this is about.'

She obeyed and a moment later he had pulled into the traffic stream.

Without taking his eyes off the road he began, 'Martin Shawcross, who manages our General Office, has just left a one-room furnished apartment in a rundown Brownstone on Lower East Side to move with his girlfriend into a newly built apartment block.

'Because the rent on his old apartment was paid until the end of the month, and there are still a few things to be moved, he kept the keys.

'When I'd briefly explained that you need somewhere to stay until you can get a flight home, he said he was quite happy for you to stay there for free until after the holiday.

'He gave me the keys, so I thought I'd drive you over now.'

'But haven't you a morning meeting scheduled?'

'Yes, but it's not until eleven o'clock, so we've time to take a quick look.'

'Oh, that's wonderful!' she exclaimed.

'You may change your mind when you've seen the place. Martin was only too glad to move out.'

The snowy street that Richard finally stopped in was lined with Brownstones and an occasional store. Though a bitter wind had sprung up a gleam of winter sun made the scene pleasant enough.

Apart from the door and the window frames needing a lick of paint the house they had drawn up in front of appeared no different from the rest.

'Well, it seems OK,' he said cautiously. 'But Martin's

apartment is on the top floor. It might be a good idea if I leave your case in the trunk until you've seen it.'

Only too aware that with a meeting looming he ought to be at the office she said, 'No, really, it'll be fine. I know it will.'

Looking unconvinced he retrieved her case and, having climbed the snowy steps, opened the door into a dark hall-way where stairs covered in the same worn brown linoleum as the floor disappeared upwards into the gloom.

Mustard-coloured paint flaked from the dingy walls and a phone that had been wrenched away from its moorings dangled forlornly. The cold air trapped in the stairwell reeked of stale cooking smells.

Richard turned back to the door. 'I really don't think this is—'

Catching his arm, Charlotte interrupted, 'Oh please… Having come this far, at least let's take a look at it.'

His mouth tight with distaste, Richard carried her case up five steep flights of stairs to the top floor landing.

A pile of old newspapers and a couple of cardboard boxes were propped against the wall and behind one of the brown-painted doors a radio was playing.

He unlocked the door at the far end and, having ushered her inside, set her case down beside a couple of small tea chests that were corded ready to go.

The air struck dank and chill as, together, they looked around the dingy room.

It was sparsely furnished with an old wardrobe, a chest of drawers, a wooden table and chair, a sagging armchair and a narrow divan that served as a bed.

A small gasfire stood on a chipped tiled hearth and on a rickety bookshelf alongside a portable television took pride of place.

On one wall was a curtained-off kitchenette and a door leading to a cramped bathroom. A grimy window overlooked the back yard trash cans and a rusty fire escape. Its ill-fitting frame was half rotten and draughts whistled through the cracks.

The radiator didn't seem to be working and there were unpleasant patches of mildew on the ceiling. In places damp paper was peeling off the walls.

'I wouldn't be happy to leave you here over Christmas,' Richard said flatly. 'For one thing it's bitterly cold. Look, let me take you to a hotel and I'll make sure the company settles the bill. Having got you over to the States, it's the very least we can do.'

But she had *wanted* to come, and if Daniel was angry when he realized what was happening and refused to let Wolfe International pay, she might be forced to foot the bill...

'There's really no need,' she said decidedly. 'This will do fine. While it isn't exactly home from home at least I'll have a room to myself...'

As he began to shake his head she added wryly, 'It has to be better than ending up in a hostel for the homeless.'

'You're a stubborn woman,' he complained, putting the keys on the table.

'I'm a grateful one.'

He pulled out his wallet. 'Well, if you're determined to stay here you'll need some money to tide you over.'

Sensing her embarrassment at having to borrow, without looking at her he put a wad of dollar bills beside the keys.

'Thank you,' she said quietly. 'I'll make sure you get it back.'

'Are you quite certain you want to stay here?'

'Quite certain.'

'Then I'd better see if I can drum up some warmth before I go.'

'Please don't make yourself late for your meeting,' she said anxiously as he set about looking for the gas meter.

Having located it in a dark cupboard he fed a number of coins into the slot before reaching for a red plastic gas-lighter lying on the hearth. After several protesting pops the fire lit with a whoosh.

'These things burn money,' he warned her, 'so you'd better make sure you've got plenty of change.'

'Thank you, I will.'

As he hesitated, clearly unwilling to leave her, she said, 'Well I mustn't keep you.'

He grinned boyishly. 'I wouldn't mind if you did. You can keep me any time you like.'

She made another attempt. 'Won't Mr Shawcross wonder where you've got to?'

'Martin will have other things on his mind. After lunch he and his girlfriend will be on their way Upstate. They're going to spend a few days with his parents, who own a hotel at Marchais.'

Glancing at his watch, he added reluctantly, 'But I suppose I'd better get off.'

'Will Daniel be at the meeting, do you know?'

'He said he'd be there.'

Urgently, she begged, 'You won't mention that you've seen me, will you?'

'Not if you don't want me to.'

'I don't.'

Seeing his fair face darken, she said, 'Please don't blame your cousin. This whole thing has been *my* fault, and now I just want to be able to go back to England and forget I've ever been to New York.'

'I'm sorry it's ended this way,' he said. Adding soberly, 'I wish things could have been different.'

So did she.

'I can't thank you enough for all the trouble you've gone to, and perhaps you'll thank Mr Shawcross for me?'

'Of course.'

'I'll drop the keys in at your reception desk as soon as I have a flight arranged.'

Green eyes glowing with gratitude, she held out her hand. 'Thank you again for all your kindness. I wish I could do something to repay it.'

He smiled at her. 'If you haven't gone home before I get back, perhaps you'll have a no-strings-attached dinner with me?'

Doing her utmost to sound enthusiastic, she agreed, 'I'd love to.'

At the door he paused. 'Oh, I almost forgot to tell you; Martin said there was plenty of clean bedding and towels in the top of the wardrobe.' A second later he was gone.

Feeling desperately alone, she stood and listened to his footsteps retreating along the landing and down the first flight of stairs.

Even with the fire lit it was still too cold to take off her outdoor things and, as she thought longingly of The Lilies, its owner's dark, handsome face filled her mind... The clear grey eyes, the jut of his cleft chin, the set of his mouth...

She would never see that face again, except perhaps in the newspapers.

All at once she was filled with such anguish that she stood transfixed, unable to move, like someone mortally wounded.

When the iron grip of misery relaxed its hold a little she told herself sternly that she couldn't go on like this. She must make an effort to put Daniel right out of her mind, along with the past, and get on with the rest of her life.

But the future looked grey and bleak. She could see no hope of happiness there.

She tried to console herself with the thought that once Christmas was over and she was back in England things would look brighter.

All she had to do was get through the next few days. Somehow.

In an attempt to keep desolation at bay, she concentrated on practicalities. There was no point in standing here shivering. While it was still daylight she would probably be warmer outside, so long as she kept on the move.

In any case she needed some supplies and, if she wasn't to freeze to death overnight, plenty of change for the gasfire.

Picking up the keys, she dropped them into her bag and, leaving the fire still burning, closed the door behind her.

It was getting dusk when she returned with a paper carrier full of provisions. Her exhaustion was bone deep and she could scarcely hold up her head as she climbed the five flights of badly-lit stairs and let herself into a room that felt icy.

As though to prove the point of Richard's words, the gasfire had gone out.

With fingers made stiff and awkward by the cold, she fumbled to feed a handful of money into the meter and relight it.

Common sense told her that, after missing lunch, she should get herself something to eat, but she had neither the strength to get it nor the appetite to want it.

After walking all afternoon, beleaguered by memories and regrets, and thoughts of Daniel, she was gripped by an iron fatigue that was almost as much mental as physical.

Moving like a very old woman, she made a cup of tea and drank it huddled in front of the fire's inadequate warmth.

There were no books to be seen and, needing some respite from the bitter-sweet memories of the previous few days, she turned on the television. After staring at an inane gameshow for a few minutes she turned it off again.

Eventually she must have dozed, because when she awoke she was stiff and her shoulders and the back of her legs were frozen.

Deciding that the warmest place would be bed, she found a towel and some bedding and made up the divan, before lifting her case on to the tea chests and unpacking her night things and a sponge bag.

The pilot-light on the bathroom geyser was out and, after a couple of unsuccessful attempts to light it, she gave up all idea of a hot shower and washed and cleaned her teeth in water so cold it made them ache.

Shivering, she undressed in front of the fire and, having turned out the light, crept beneath the blankets still wearing her dressing-gown.

Her feet were icy cold and she lay listening to the bubbling hiss of the fire and the wind whistling through the gaps in the window frame, wrapped in her own loneliness like a moth in a cocoon.

Then, in one of the neighbouring apartments, the sound of a carol being sung reminded her that tomorrow was Christmas Eve. If things had been different she would have been going up to the Catskills with Daniel.

That was when the futile tears came.

Once the floodgates had opened she cried for a long time. The night was almost over before she slipped into a fitful doze that, plagued by too many unhappy dreams, brought her little real rest.

When she opened her eyes, for a few seconds she was totally disorientated before memory painted in the gloomy picture of loss and a Christmas spent alone.

But, as though the previous night she had plumbed the depths and the only way left was up, her natural fighting spirit re-asserted itself.

She *wouldn't* give way to self pity, she told herself

fiercely. At least she had a roof over her head. Friends. She was a lot luckier than some.

Loving Daniel Wolfe was an aberration, a madness that would eventually pass.

Even if he hadn't been a womanizing swine and responsible for Tim's death, it would never have worked. They were poles apart and always would be.

He had badly affected her life in the past, but she wasn't going to allow this futile longing for him to wreck the future.

A glance at her watch showed it was already noon and, trying to put Daniel right out of her mind, Charlotte left the almost-warmth of her bed and, picking up the gas lighter, made her way into the dingy bathroom.

After a short tussle she managed to re-light the geyser, then went to make herself a cup of tea.

Seized by a sudden restlessness of spirit, she couldn't wait to get out into the street and, huddled against the fire, she drank her tea quickly.

Then, having fished in her case for fresh underwear and her warmest clothes, she ventured to take a shower.

She soon discovered that the flow of water was erratic, and the temperature veered between tepid and scalding hot. Added to that, the shower-head was broken and she couldn't direct it properly, which meant her hair got saturated and she was forced to wash it. Still, it was a shower of sorts and more than welcome.

Despite the rising steam the air in the tiny bathroom was uncomfortably cold and the moment she turned off the water she started to shiver.

Fastening a towel round her head, she hurried back to dry herself in front of the fire.

It had started to snow again. Big feathery flakes were being swirled past the window by a brisk wind, and the air coming through the chinks felt icy.

If the weather proved too inclement, Charlotte decided, she would take refuge in one or other of the big stores. She might even treat herself to a spot of late lunch, as it was Christmas Eve…

Christmas Eve…

Daniel would be on his way to the Catskills by now. Maybe he had taken Janice…

Feeling sick and hollow inside, she pulled on her underwear. She was about to start drying her hair when the knock came.

It was so unexpected that she jumped.

Her heart suddenly picking up speed, she wondered who on earth could it be? The only person who knew she was here was Richard, and he was in Florida…

Apart from Martin Shawcross, of course. He might have popped round to pick up something, or to see how she was.

Sighing at her own foolishness, she pulled on her dressing-gown and, tying the belt tightly, went to answer the knock.

CHAPTER SEVEN

THE door was half open before she recalled that Richard had said Martin Shawcross was going Upstate. Even so, the man standing there was the last person she had expected to see and for a second or two she simply gaped at him foolishly.

Daniel… Daniel was here.

Instead of taking Janice to the Catskills he had come looking for her.

Her very being took wing.

She was euphoric, high on happiness, when her seesaw suddenly came down to earth with a bump.

Seized by a kind of despairing anger, she realized that his being here didn't change a thing.

It didn't alter the fact that, by falling in love with him, she had betrayed her brother. It didn't alter the fact that he was still having an affair with Janice. It didn't alter the past or mean he cared a jot about her.

She made a belated attempt to shut the door in his face but she had left it far too late. Anticipating the move, his foot was in the way.

A moment later she found herself swept back inside and the door closed after them.

His grey eyes hard, his mouth set, he leaned his shoulders against the panels and folded his arms. Flakes of snow had settled on the collar of his car coat and were melting on his dark hair.

Her heart thudding like a trip-hammer, she asked thickly, 'What do you want? Why are you here?'

'Why do you think?'

His bleak expression, as much as his words, made it clear that he had come because he was angry at the way she had walked out without a word.

'How did you know where to find me?'

'Does it matter?' He sounded almost weary.

Then, with a wry twist to his lips, 'If you're blaming Richard for giving you away, you're wrong. He didn't say a word about seeing you.'

Grimly, he added, 'If he had, it wouldn't have taken me so long to track you down.'

'I asked him not to,' she admitted.

'I rather thought that might be the case.'

Lifting her chin, she said, 'So now you have *tracked me down* I suppose you want an apology?'

As her eyes met his she realized with a sinking feeling that he was absolutely furious. But his voice was quiet as he said, 'An apology wouldn't come amiss, but I want a great deal more than that.'

'The money back you've spent on me?'

'You'll stop being so sassy, unless you want me to turn you over my knee and spank you.'

As she recoiled from the softly-spoken threat the towel turban she was wearing slipped drunkenly over one ear.

A wintry gleam of amusement appeared in his eyes.

Pulling the towel free and shaking her still-damp hair loose, she faced him with what dignity she could muster. 'I'm sorry, I shouldn't have said that.'

'No, you shouldn't.'

Taking a deep breath, she went on with polite formality, 'You've been very kind to me, and I hope you'll forgive me for leaving so abruptly.'

'Bravo!' he said caustically.

'Well, what more do you want?' she demanded, hiding her fear behind a screen of bravado.

'As I've just said, a great deal. Including the answers to

a lot of questions. Such as *why* you ran away without a word, and what made you decide to go back to England?'

So he knew about that.

'But they can wait for another time. At the moment I want to get moving. The forecast is for blizzard conditions, and we've a longish way to go.'

As she stared at him he reminded her crisply, 'If you recall, you agreed to spend Christmas in the Catskills with me.'

In spite of everything, for an instant she was sorely tempted.

Made foolish by love and a longing she still couldn't banish, she tried to tell herself that if she could only have a little more time in his company, see his face, hear his voice, just *be* with him, she could keep everything under control.

But almost immediately common sense warned her that she couldn't. Magnetically drawn to him as she was, it would be like carrying a flaming torch into a dynamite store.

Shaking her head, she said stiffly, 'I've changed my mind.'

He raised a dark brow. 'Really?'

'I don't want to spend Christmas with you there, or anywhere else for that matter,' she went on firmly.

Knowing he was taking the biggest gamble of his life, he laid it on the line. 'At the risk of sounding ungentlemanly, I have to tell you that in the circumstances it's what *I* want that counts... So if you'd like to start putting on your clothes... Unless you want me to do it for you?'

Her breath coming fast, she informed him, 'No, I most certainly do not!'

'Then I'll give you five minutes to dry your hair and get dressed.'

Stubbornly she shook her head. 'I don't need to get dressed. I'm not going anywhere.'

He shrugged. 'Very well.'

She thought she'd won until, straightening up, he moved towards her purposefully.

There was something so formidable about him that, saying distractedly, 'Leave me alone,' she backed away until the chair stopped her. 'I've told you I'm not going anywhere.'

Ignoring her protest, he started to unfasten the belt of her dressing-gown.

Feeling half-suffocated and desperately trying to push his hands away she protested, 'I don't want you to dress me.'

'I was thinking more of *undressing* you.'

Opening the lapels of her dressing-gown, he ran a fingertip beneath the lacy edge of her bra cups, making her shudder convulsively.

'I imagine the warmest place in this God-forsaken hole is bed, and if we aren't going anywhere we'll need to do something to pass the time.

'If you've plenty of supplies at hand—' he went on thoughtfully '—we'll hardly need to get out of bed until Christmas is over.'

Pulling away, panic-stricken now, she cried, 'If you don't get out of here this very minute, I'll start screaming.'

'Dear me,' he said mildly, 'we can't have the neighbours disturbed.'

A moment later his mouth was covering hers.

She tried to struggle but, holding her easily, he carried on kissing her until she was dazed and breathless and her legs were like water.

Then, his voice sardonic, he asked, 'Still think screaming's an option?'

Shaken to the very soul, she whispered, 'I don't want to spend Christmas with you. I don't want anything to do with you. You're a brute and a beast and a devil and I'd sooner—'

A finger to her lips, stopping the flow of words, he said, 'You can call me all the names you like later but right now it's decision time.'

She jerked her head back and looked away, trembling from head to toe.

Watching her half-averted face he asked, 'So what's it to be? Christmas in the Catskills, or here?'

As she hesitated, wondering if he might be bluffing and trying desperately to think of some way out, he remarked, 'To tell you the truth, I'm getting to quite like the idea of staying here…'

Advancing, as she steered round the chair and backed away, he added, 'It'll save a long drive and I must admit that I can't wait to make love to you again.'

As the edge of the divan caught her behind the knees and she sat down abruptly he pulled a phone from his pocket. 'The only problem is, though I've plenty of clothes and everything I need up at the lodge, I haven't even a toothbrush here. So I'll have to ring Mrs Morgan and ask her to—'

'Wait!' Charlotte cried. 'If I agree to go with you, will you promise not to touch me?'

'No,' he said bluntly. 'But I promise not to try and force you in any way. Whether you go to bed with me or not will be up to you.'

That option, while she recognized the risks involved all too clearly, had to be the best.

'Very well… I'll come.'

'Then we'd better have that hair dried first,' Daniel said matter-of-factly. 'Is there a fresh towel anywhere?'

'In the top of the wardrobe.' She made to get up.

'Stay where you are. I'll get it.' He came back a few seconds later with a pale green hand towel.

Her breathing restricted and her heart feeling as though it was too big for her chest, she sat perfectly still while he began to rub her hair, gently but thoroughly.

When it was dried to his satisfaction he queried laconically, 'Brush?'

'In the bathroom.'

Returning with it in his hand, he brushed out the tangles, watching the red-gold mass ripple beneath the long, smooth strokes.

At length, he put down the brush and said, 'That should be fine.'

'Thank you.' Her voice sounded unsteady.

'It was my pleasure,' he assured her mockingly.

When she started to coil it up he stopped her. 'Leave it down; I prefer it that way.'

Too emotionally fraught to argue, and shivering with a combination of cold and nervous reaction, she pulled on the rest of her clothes as quickly as possible before repacking her few belongings.

As soon as her case was fastened Daniel picked it up and, having collected the keys, turned out the gas fire and led the way to the door.

'What were you going to do about the keys?' he asked as they started down the stairs.

'I said I'd leave them at your reception desk.'

He dropped them into his pocket. 'In that case, I'll give them back to Martin Shawcross when I see him.'

Outside, the sidewalk was carpeted in white once more and large flakes of snow were being swirled along by an icy wind.

Charlotte, expecting to find the limousine waiting for them with Perkins at the wheel, was surprised to see a sturdy dark blue four-wheel drive Traveller drawn up by the kerb.

'This is my bad weather transport,' Daniel explained briefly.

He tossed her case in the back and, having helped her climb into the front passenger seat, jumped in beside her.

A moment later they were off, fat, fuzzy flakes of snow landing on the windscreen like lacy spiders, only to be brushed away seconds later by the wipers.

For a while they drove in silence, while Daniel concentrated on the traffic and Charlotte tried to sort out her jumbled thoughts and emotions.

She felt scared and agitated, full of uncertainty and confusion. Why had he forced her into keeping the arrangement? Was it merely to have his own way? Or a determination to punish her for the way she had treated him?

The latter almost certainly. There was a kind of slow-burning anger in him, an anger he would want to vent in some way.

But it wouldn't be physical, she felt sure of that. There was nothing crude about Daniel; he had finesse and subtlety, a tactical mind that scared her stiff.

Shivering inwardly, she faced the fact that instead of being empty and lonely, as she had expected, the next few days would be fraught.

For instance, when he got round to demanding answers to his questions, what was she to tell him?

Certainly not the truth.

If he discovered how she felt about him it would no doubt suit him nicely to lure her into his bed and then, when the holiday was over, dump her and have the last laugh.

So she mustn't let him discover it.

And she must find some defence against her own feelings. If she didn't she was in line for even more heartbreak.

She thought with despair that she had expected to ex-

perience the agony of parting only once. Now it would be
twice over.

All this pain for a man who wasn't worth it! How had
she come to give her heart and body and soul to someone
like Daniel? she wondered helplessly.

If only he hadn't managed to find her, to stir everything
up again.

But he had, and the only way she could cope with this
enforced trip to the Catskills would be to treat the whole
thing as prosaically as possible.

That meant getting back on some kind of, if not *friendly*
footing, then at least civil.

Surreptitiously, she studied his profile. It was lean and
clean cut, with features that would make him a pleasure to
look at even when he was old.

As though aware of her scrutiny, he gave her a sidelong
glance.

Feeling her colour rise, she looked hastily away.

They had left Manhattan behind them and were heading
Upstate when, plucking up her courage, she cleared her
throat and asked, 'How much longer will the journey take?'

Looking at the snowflakes, which were smaller now and
falling faster, he said, 'Hard to say. A couple of hours or
so, depending on the conditions.'

'Where exactly is the lodge?'

'Halfway up a mountain on the outskirts of a small village known as Hailstone Creek.'

'How big is it?'

'Not very. Three bedrooms, a couple of bathrooms, a
living-room and kitchen; all very simple.'

'You say it was the family home?'

'Hailstone Lodge was the family's *holiday* home but, as
the place held a lot of happy memories and I was fond of
it, I decided to keep it.'

'So you didn't actually live at the lodge?'

'No, we lived in Albany. Both my sister and I were born and bred there, and only moved away when we went to college.

'Throughout our childhood we used to go up to the lodge to hike in the summer and ski in the winter.'

'I went skiing once on a school trip,' Charlotte said, 'and thoroughly enjoyed it. But the nursery slopes would be a far cry from the Catskills.'

'Well, it's a start,' he said. 'And, once you have the basics, cross-country skiing can be fun…'

For a while they conversed politely then, giving up the struggle, Charlotte relapsed into silence and watched the scenery while she tried to think what she would say when the showdown finally came.

The weather was worsening by the time he stopped at a small roadside restaurant, saying, 'I thought we could use a drink.'

Inside the steamy diner he asked, 'Would you like anything to eat?'

Her appetite non-existent, she shook her head.

'Did you have any lunch?'

'No,' she admitted. 'But I'm really not hungry.'

While they sipped their coffee, his dark face withdrawn, Daniel said nothing and Charlotte wondered if he was already regretting his decision to make her come.

If he hadn't been so set on punishing her he could no doubt have spent the holiday wrapped in the welcoming embrace of any number of women.

Janice for one, she thought bitterly.

By the time they resumed their journey the scenery was shrouded by driving veils of white, and a keening wind was throwing handfuls of snow and torn-off twigs at the windscreen like a child in a tantrum.

Despite the conditions Daniel kept going steadily and, after a while, tired from the previous night's lack of sleep, comfortably warm and half-hypnotised by the rhythmic shush of the wipers, Charlotte dozed.

When she awoke it was dark and they seemed to be climbing steadily, their headlights moving over the swirling curtain of snow like the searching antennae of some insect.

Sitting up straighter, she rubbed the back of her neck and peered through the windscreen. She could see no sign of a road, just a ragged line of snow-covered trees on either side.

'We've just passed Marchais,' Daniel said, 'so it's not far now.'

'I'm glad about that,' she answered fervently. 'You must be driving by guess and by God.'

His smile wry, he admitted, 'It's just as well I know the road.'

They had covered about half a mile when he turned right through a gap in the trees and a moment later yellow lights shone a welcome through the blizzard.

When he stopped the car she saw that the lodge appeared to be a single-storey timbered building with a covered front porch. Its shingled roof was steeply pitched and pale grey smoke from one of its chimneys was writhing through the blown snow like an escaping genie.

'Wait here a minute,' Daniel instructed and, jumping out, climbed the porch steps to open the door. He was back almost immediately to put an arm around Charlotte's waist and hurry her through the biting wind and snow.

A little flurry of snowflakes was blown in with them, which straight away began to melt in the brightness and warmth of the living-room.

Having fetched her case he set it down on a bench and, taking her coat, shook it before hanging it in a floor-to-ceiling cupboard. Then, heading for the door again, he said, 'Make yourself at home while I put the car away.'

Suddenly, noticing how strained and weary his face was, she asked impulsively, 'Do you have to put it away?'

'I think it would be preferable to having to dig it out if it keeps on snowing.'

When the door had closed behind him she glanced around. The room was pleasant and spacious, with honey-coloured walls, wax-polished floorboards and the minimum of simple furniture.

As well as the radiators a log fire was burning in the grate, and over the mantelpiece hung a decorated spruce bough. To one side of the fireplace a large basket held a supply of split logs and kindling and a nearby alcove was stacked with logs.

There were heavy folkweave curtains in shades of cream and russet and a couch and several easy chairs upholstered in the same material. A lovely old grandmother clock ticked solemnly.

Any faint notion she might have harboured about roughing it somewhere out in the wilds disappeared.

A faint but appetizing smell of cooking was coming from a door at the end.

Opening it, Charlotte found a cosy, old-fashioned kitchen with pegged rugs, pine furniture and a couple of comfortable-looking armchairs drawn up in front of a glowing black stove.

On one side of the stove a Dutch cooking pot was simmering gently and on the other a metal coffee jug was standing on a trivet. Waiting on the warming rack were two large earthenware bowls.

Though Daniel had mentioned a Mrs Munroe there was no sign of any housekeeper or caretaker.

As the thought went through her mind she heard the front door open and close again and a moment later Daniel came through to the kitchen. He had taken off his coat and was wearing a black crew-necked sweater.

Crossing to the stove, he held out his hands to the warmth. Snow was melting on his dark hair and, as she watched, a drop trickled down his cheek. He wiped it away with the back of his hand.

Firelight shone on his face, turning it to bronze, and picking out the planes and hollows. With the skin stretched taut over the hard bone structure and his mouth set, he looked bleak and formidable. Nothing like the smiling man she had grown used to.

Taking a deep breath she said, 'Though there's a meal ready on the stove I haven't seen anything of Mrs Munroe.'

'You won't.'

'She doesn't live here?'

'No, she lives about a mile further along the track. With the weather getting worse, I should imagine she went home as soon as possible.'

So they were alone.

Tendrils of something suspiciously like fear curling in her stomach, Charlotte found herself babbling, 'In all this snow it must be equally difficult whether you're driving or walking.'

Coolly he said, 'I understand that Mrs Munroe lived in Maine before she got married and moved to New York State, so she's used to plenty of snow. Ten to one she came over on their snowmobile.'

'Oh, I see... I've never been on a snowmobile, but I should imagine it's enormous fun.'

'Enormous,' he agreed drily. 'If you'd like to have a go tomorrow there's a Snowcat in the garage.'

'I'd love to.'

'But for now, as neither of us have had any lunch, suppose we eat?'

'Of course...' Glancing at the table, which was already set with cutlery and a basket of crusty bread, she asked awkwardly, 'Shall I dish up?'

He answered ironically, 'As you're my guest, albeit an unwilling one, I'll do the honours.'

Sitting down at the table, she watched him take the lid from the pot and, with a large metal ladle, fill the two bowls with steaming chunks of savoury meat and vegetables.

Setting one in front of her he said, 'Tuck in. Though it's rather unusual fare for a Christmas Eve, you'll find Mrs Munroe makes an excellent stew.'

Still with no appetite, Charlotte reluctantly picked up a fork. After a couple of mouthfuls, suddenly finding she was ravenously hungry, she began to eat with delicate greed, clearing her plate and mopping up the gravy with a hunk of homemade bread.

When she looked up, Daniel was watching her.

His face stern, he asked, 'When did you last eat?'

Flushing, she answered, 'I'm not quite sure.'

'When?'

'Breakfast time.'

'This morning?'

'Yesterday morning,' she admitted.

He muttered something under his breath that could have been an oath before saying grimly, 'Not eating for so long is absolutely idiotic! Why the devil—?' He broke off abruptly.

Then, after a moment, regaining control, he continued more quietly, 'But we'll talk *after* we've finished our meal.'

Rising to his feet, he went to the warming oven and returned with a pie, the pastry of which was crisp and golden.

When he had taken two clean bowls from the dresser and a carton of cream from the fridge, server in hand, he asked, 'You'll have some, won't you?'

Unconsciously playing for time, she asked, 'What kind of pie is it?'

'Apple.'

'How do you know?'

He grinned briefly. 'Mrs Munroe is nothing if not consistent. She's been leaving me the same meal for as long as I can remember. But her apple pie, like her stew, is absolutely first class.'

'Then I will have some, please.'

He cut two sizable chunks and poured a liberal helping of cream on to both of them.

Accepting her dish, Charlotte tried for lightness. 'Don't tell me, the last one to finish does the washing up?'

'Happily, there's a dishwasher lurking behind that cupboard door. However, the last one to finish can stack it and pour the coffee.'

With no inclination to hurry, Charlotte was easily the last. While he went into the living-room, she cleared away the dirty dishes, found milk in the larder-fridge and filled two mugs with steaming coffee.

When she carried them through, Daniel had made up the fire and was just closing the curtains. The snowy night shut out, he returned to sit on the couch in front of the blazing hearth.

He seemed to have come to some kind of decision, and there was a glint in his eye, an air of *purpose* about him that was disturbing, to say the least.

Her stomach feeling as though it was full of agitated butterflies, she set the mugs down on the coffee table and hovered uncertainly, wishing she was anywhere but there.

Now it was too late a belated return to common sense told her that Daniel had almost certainly been bluffing. She should have refused to come, she realized, and called that bluff.

His little smile suggesting that he knew exactly what she was thinking and feeling, and that he was enjoying her alarm, he reached for one of the mugs and, glancing up at her from beneath long thick lashes, asked, 'Afraid I'll bite if you get too close?'

'Of course not.' In spite of all her efforts, her voice wobbled.

He patted the couch beside him. 'Then why don't you come and sit down?'

She sat down, choosing the chair furthest away, and saw the corner of his long, mobile mouth twitch.

'Taking no chances, I see.'

Ignoring that remark, she stared into the fire, watching little flames lick the logs with cats' tongues while she wondered desperately how she was going to get through the rest of the evening with her woefully inadequate defences intact.

Of course an early night would help.

Pretending to stifle a yawn she said, 'I'm afraid I didn't get much sleep last night. It was too cold... So, if you don't mind, I'd like to go to bed before too long.'

'That sounds like a very good idea,' he agreed blandly. 'But first I want you to tell me what made you leave so suddenly?'

'I—I don't want to talk about it.'

'As you were living in my house, and had slept in my bed, don't you think I've a right to know?'

Biting her lip, she said nothing.

Quietly, he asked, 'Have you any idea how I felt when I woke up and found you'd gone?'

When she still remained silent, putting his mug down, he pinned her with cool grey eyes. 'Didn't it ever occur to you that I might be worried to death?'

She had presumed that he would be vexed, angry at the way she'd left, but she hadn't expected him to be seriously worried.

'Well, didn't it?' he insisted.

'No, it didn't.' Then, defensively, 'I'm a grown woman, not a child.'

'A grown woman you undoubtedly are, but that didn't

stop you *behaving* like a child,' he said curtly. 'In fact, any child would have had more sense than to deliberately half-starve itself. I was right to be concerned about you.'

'I didn't deliberately half-starve myself. Somehow I just wasn't hungry.'

He sighed. 'Tell me, Charlotte, what made you run like a frightened rabbit?'

Lifting her chin, she informed him haughtily, 'I've no intention of discussing it.'

A glint in his eye, he remarked, 'I see... A rabbit with attitude. So, what made you run?'

Knowing only too well that he wouldn't give up until he had an answer, she admitted, 'I realized I should never have come.'

'I thought you liked New York.'

'I do.'

'So it was *me* you didn't like?'

'I didn't want to get involved.'

'Why not?'

In desperation she said, 'I've never gone in for brief flings or sleeping with the boss.'

'So why did you?'

'I don't know... It just happened.'

'You must have been attracted,' he pursued. 'Otherwise you *wouldn't* have slept with me.'

'I wish I hadn't!'

'Didn't you enjoy it?'

She wanted to say no, but couldn't.

Watching the colour rise in her cheeks, he asked, 'But you woke up blaming me for what had happened?'

'No,' she whispered. 'I was equally to blame.'

'We're both healthy, consenting adults, so why are we talking about *blame*?'

'Because it *shouldn't* have happened.'

'Why shouldn't it?' he probed.

'I've already told you. Sleeping with the boss just isn't my scene.'

As her face grew even more flushed he said quietly, 'But the fact that you behaved differently this time doesn't mean that you had to leave.'

She shook her head. 'What happened made my position untenable.'

'Well, even if you woke up and regretted the whole thing it was the height of stupidity to run like you did.

'Why didn't you talk to me about it? Tell me what you were thinking of doing? Or were you afraid I'd persuade you to stay after all?'

Her expression was answer enough.

'If you'd *truly* regretted what had happened, and didn't want to compromise your position in the company, I would have understood and kept well out of your way.'

Seriously, he added, 'I wouldn't dream of putting pressure on an unwilling woman.'

'That's a laugh!' She fought back. 'You forced me to come up here with you when I didn't want to.'

'Why didn't you want to? Were you scared that if you did you'd weaken and sleep with me again?'

'No,' she lied hardily. 'The whole thing was a terrible mistake. And I've no intention of making the same mistake twice.'

'I see.' His voice was smooth as silk. 'In that case you should be safe enough. Tell me, Charlotte—'

Jumping to her feet, she broke in hoarsely, 'I don't want to answer any more questions. I'd like to go to bed, if you'll show me where I'm sleeping?'

'You don't want to stay up for a while, as it's Christmas Eve?'

Knowing breaking-point was close, and desperate to be on her own, she insisted, 'No, I'd prefer to go *now*, if you don't mind.'

'Very well.'

Uncoiling his long length from the couch, he ushered her through a door to the left, where a bedside lamp was burning.

Once again the furniture was simple and sparse, but there was a big double divan made up with soft pillows and a cosy duvet.

While she looked around her he carried her case in and put it down on a wooden chest. Then, closing the door, he set his back against it and smiled at her.

That smile made her throat and mouth go dry.

CHAPTER EIGHT

WHILE she stood and stared at him, her heart beating so fast she could hardly breathe, he stripped off his sweater and tossed it on to a nearby chair. Beneath it he was wearing a maroon silk shirt and a striped tie.

Loosening the knot in his tie, he pulled it from around his neck and, coiling it neatly, dropped it on to the dressing table before starting to unbutton his shirt cuffs.

'What are you doing?' she demanded unsteadily.

He raised a dark brow before answering precisely, 'Unbuttoning my shirt cuffs.'

'Why are you getting undressed?'

'I usually do before I go to bed.'

'But you can't sleep in here!' she cried.

'It happens to be my room,' he informed her mildly.

'Then I'd like another room... A room of my own,' she insisted, her green eyes filled with alarm.

'As I usually come here alone I'm afraid there's only one bedroom in use,' he told her, his voice regretful, 'so we'll just have to manage.

'Still, we have slept together before, when all's said and done, so it's no big deal.'

'It might not be for you,' she protested hoarsely, 'but I don't want to sleep in the same bed. I want to sleep alone... And you said you wouldn't touch me.'

He shook his head. 'I promised not to try and force you in any way. A promise I intend to keep. And you've just assured me that you have no intention of making the same mistake twice...'

132

Grey eyes gleaming between thick lashes, he added, 'So, unless you're not sure you can trust yourself...?'

'I'm quite sure.'

He spread his hands palms upwards, 'Then we don't have a problem. If we each keep to our own side of the bed it will be as good as sleeping alone.'

As though it was all settled, he began to undo his shirt buttons. When it was unfastened he tugged it free from his trousers and sent it to follow his sweater.

His clear olive skin glowed like oiled silk in the lamp-light, and in helpless fascination she watched the smooth ripple of chest and shoulder muscles as he reached to un-fasten the clip on his waistband.

He was sliding down the zip when her nerve broke. Turning, she fled into the bathroom, followed by his soft laughter.

The devil had planned this, she thought furiously. It was part of her punishment to be made to sleep in the same bed.

Unless she could think of some way out of it.

Had there been a bolt on the bathroom door, though it seemed silly and humiliating and cowardly, she might well have bolted it and refused to come out.

But there wasn't. Which meant he could walk in any time he chose to... *If* he chose to...

Abstractedly opening a cupboard door, she found a pile of soft towels and a shelf well stocked with toilet articles.

Having helped herself to a bottle of shower-gel, a tube of toothpaste, a cellophane-wrapped toothbrush and a comb she cleaned her teeth, showered and combed out her tangled hair while she tried to decide what to do for the best.

She could keep fighting, of course. But that was probably what he was. *expecting* her to do, so would she be playing into his hands?

He was a master tactician. If he could keep her flustered,

off balance, it would give him an advantage and her less chance to stay in control.

And stay in control she must. If she once lost her head she would be at his mercy.

So might it not be best to accept the situation quietly and keep her cool?

He had said he wouldn't pressure her so that left only her own feelings to guard against and knowing about Janice was a big help. That additional proof of what he was like should make it a great deal easier to flip the coin and hate him…

Her night things were still in her case and she put a large towel around herself, sarong-wise, and tucked the end in before opening the door a crack and peering into the bedroom.

Though Daniel's clothes remained where he had discarded them, the big bed was unoccupied and there was no sign of him.

The door to the living-room was ajar and, peeping in, she saw that too was empty, though a spark-guard had been placed in front of the fire.

Realizing that he was probably using the second bathroom, she went over to her case to look for a nightdress and dressing-gown.

A kind of perverse pride made her take out the set that Carla had bought her for her birthday—a cream satin nightdress with multiple spaghetti shoulder straps and a matching negligée—saying firmly, 'It's high time you had something glamorous'.

She was just about to pull the nightdress over her head when Daniel walked in wearing a short towelling robe, his thick dark hair still damp from the shower.

Feeling her towel start to slip, and made clumsy by haste, she put an arm through one set of straps.

For several undignified seconds she tried to hold the towel with one hand while she struggled to free herself.

'You'd better let me help,' Daniel said, straight faced, and made to take the towel.

The nightdress still tangled around her neck, and terrified of what might happen next, Charlotte batted his hand away and clutched the towel to her.

Grinning openly now, he advised, 'You'd do better to let go. You'll strangle yourself if you carry on like this.'

Knowing who she *would* like to strangle, she hissed, 'Go away and leave me alone.'

'Certain you wouldn't like any help?

'Quite certain!' she said through gritted teeth.

Rather to her surprise, he turned and went, closing the door behind him.

All at once she felt curiously deflated.

Infuriated by her own stupidity, she sorted herself out and, not knowing quite what else to do, had just got into bed when there was a discreet knock.

A second later Daniel put his head round the door and queried, 'All fixed?'

'Yes, thank you,' she said stiffly.

His air casual, he came round to her side of the bed and sat on the edge.

Sitting up abruptly she demanded, 'What are you doing?'

'There's no need to panic.'

'I'm not panicking,' she lied.

'Strange, that's what it looks like.'

'You said you'd keep to your half of the bed,' she reminded him.

'I've changed my mind about that…' He left the sentence in mid-air. As her eyes widened he burst out laughing. 'You should just see your face!'

'You're a swine!' she said hoarsely.

He looked hurt. 'How can you revile me when I've decided to be nice to you?'

'I don't *want* you to be nice to me,' she told him, her voice tight.

'Well, if that's how you feel… But, as you seemed so against sharing a bed, I thought I'd sleep on the couch in front of the fire…

'Though, of course if you really don't want me to…'

'I *do*.'

'Well, that's positive enough, if a shade unflattering.'

Only too aware that he might be deliberately baiting her, Charlotte held her breath and waited for him to go.

When he got to his feet and turned away, in spite of everything, she had to fight a strong urge to beg him to stay.

His hand was on the knob of the door before he suddenly said, 'But I'm forgetting something,' and came back.

'What?' she whispered through a dry throat as he sat on the bed once more.

'You haven't kissed me goodnight.'

'I don't *want* to kiss you goodnight.'

'Now, is that nice? When I'm willing to spend an uncomfortable night on the couch just so you won't be tempted.'

Ignoring that provocative remark, she repeated desperately, 'I don't want to kiss you.'

'Okay,' he agreed accommodatingly, '*I'll* kiss *you*. That way your conscience will be clear.' He smiled into her eyes.

He only had to look at her to unlock her mind and turn it towards him, while every single nerve in her body came alive and every muscle tensed at the sexual promise implicit in that smile.

Leaning forward, he kissed her on the mouth. His kiss was delicate, full of beauty and magic and sensuousness, and more welcome than cool water to someone dying of thirst in the desert.

As her lips parted helplessly beneath the light pressure of his he kissed her a second time, longer, sweeter, deeper, while running his hands up and down her slender back.

Holding her head between his palms, he kissed her face, her forehead and cheeks, her closed eyelids. Then, his mouth on hers once more, he began to caress her breasts, cupping their soft weight, teasing the nipples through the satin of her nightdress.

She gave a little gasp.

Raising his head he said huskily, 'If you still want me to go, tell me now.'

Though limp and dazed with wanting him, she tried to hold on to sanity. 'Yes, I...'

He was drawing away when the longing to have him stay, the hunger for him, overwhelmed her. Her arms going round his neck, she whispered, 'No, don't go.'

With a sound almost like a sigh he shrugged out of his robe and, slipping into bed beside her, drew her close.

He felt so good to her. Her face buried against his neck, she touched her lips to the hollow at the base of his throat, sensing that his heart rate picked up and gathered speed.

The now familiar scent of him engulfed her and with her tongue-tip she enjoyed the clean, slightly salty taste of his skin.

He ran a hand down the length of her body, over her waist and hip and thigh, then back across her flat stomach and her ribcage, to her breasts.

The thin satin was suddenly a barrier that neither of them wanted and, her fingers unsteady, she helped him remove it.

'That's better,' he said softly and once again traced her slim body with his hand, loving the feel of her, the womanliness of her.

Then, his mouth at her breast, his long fingers found and stroked the silky skin of her inner thighs, pleasuring her until she began to make little sounds deep in her throat.

There was so much pent-up emotion in her she thought that if he didn't make love to her soon she would die of it.

Kissing her neck, where her hair was lying in silky red-gold tendrils, he brushed it back, spreading it over the white pillow.

'Please,' she whispered.

He hesitated and she said again more urgently, 'Oh please, Daniel…'

While he lowered himself on to her, slowly, with such restraint, she gazed up at him, her green eyes sparkling, a look in them that almost made him lose control.

Oh, I love him so much, she thought as she arched herself towards him, welcoming his weight.

Knowing he had never wanted any other woman like he wanted this one, he smiled and kissed her lips.

He was powerful physically but he used his strength gently, whispering soft words into her ear as he loved her, telling her how beautiful she was, how much he wanted her.

As they both swung high in the cradle of desire he made love to her for a long time without tiring, amazing her with his stamina, carrying her to the heights again and again, while he murmured her name like a mantra, an incantation.

The sheer magnetism of it held her mind still while her body shuddered against his.

At last they lay quietly, while their breathing eased and they drifted slowly back to earth still caressing each other. She, stroking the nape of his neck, her fingertips ruffling his hair and tracing the strong tendons. He, turning his head to kiss her cheek and nip her ear lobe with his teeth.

When her stomach clenched in response he noticed the

slight but unmistakable reaction and she felt him smile in the semi-darkness.

Though he had done nothing overtly to dominate her he had dominated her completely and she had welcomed it, like a tigress would welcome a graceful, powerful mate.

But it went far beyond the physical. It was as though he'd taken possession of her very soul.

Overwhelmed by the sheer enormity of it, she began to cry. She didn't make a sound and the tears ran silently down her cheeks, but still he knew at once and began to kiss them away.

Finally, held in his arms, her cheek fitted into the slight dip in the middle of his chest, his chin resting on her hair, she slept.

When Charlotte awoke the room was full of snowy light and she was alone in the bed. A glance at her watch showed it was almost midday and there wasn't a whisper of sound.

Sitting up with clammy palms and a hammering heart, she wondered, what if he'd made love to her last night just to get his own back and then gone quietly away and left her, as she'd left him?

She felt a desolation of spirit so great that she moaned aloud. But this was just the beginning of her pain, her punishment for falling in love with a Lothario.

Even if he hadn't gone now, that was what it would come to in the end.

But what was she to do *now*, in the immediate future?

Having burnt her boats by coming up here with him, she could see no alternative but to stick it out. Though that didn't mean she had to sleep with him again. If she could find the strength to say no and mean it he would take no for an answer.

Last night, after turning on the heat, he had hesitated, as

though he himself had doubts about the wisdom of what they were doing.

Perhaps he had thought Janice might be jealous and, if Janice was the woman he was thinking of marrying... But if she *was*, why wasn't he with her now?

It didn't make sense.

But what did?

Charlotte felt as though she was on a frail, careening rope bridge stretched across an abyss.

Getting out of bed, she went through to the bathroom where she showered, cleaned her teeth and combed her hair again like an automaton.

She was returning to the bedroom to find some fresh clothes when the door opened and Daniel walked in. He was still wearing his robe.

From across the room he eyed her nakedness with approval. 'You look like some woodland nymph.'

'I was just about to get dressed,' she said, snatching up her negligée.

'I've got a better idea; come here and give me a kiss and then get back into bed.'

Standing her ground, she half shook her head. 'I can't...'

'Of course you can,' he said cheerfully. 'I thought, as it's Christmas Day, we could have brunch in bed.'

'Oh...'

'It needn't stop at brunch, if you're disappointed?'

'I'm not,' she denied hastily.

'Pity. Still, come and give me that kiss.'

When she stood as if rooted to the spot he threatened, 'Do I have to come and get you?'

'Please, Daniel,' she whispered.

Seeing the helpless anguish in her eyes he said slowly, 'So last night changed nothing?'

'Did you expect it to?'

'Perhaps not,' he admitted. 'There are still too many things we haven't yet thrashed out.'

Then, briskly, 'But with brunch waiting this isn't the time to do it. Would you rather eat in bed or in front of the stove?'

'In front of the stove.' She made her choice without a moment's hesitation.

'Very well. The stove it is.'

As soon as he'd gone she pulled on her underwear, a pair of navy trousers and an Aran jumper and, having braced herself, went through to the kitchen.

Daniel had dressed too, and was wearing a dark polo-necked sweater and casual trousers.

Waving her to one of the chairs drawn up to a cheerful blaze, he handed her a napkin, a fork, and a plate before bringing a dish full of food from the warming oven.

'Simple, but tasty, I hope.'

There were boiled eggs cut in half, their orange yolks just gooey, crisp little rolls of bacon, small sausages, corn scallops, hash browns, baby tomatoes, button mushrooms, and re-fried beans.

Servers in hand, he queried, 'I'll give you a bit of everything, shall I?'

Before she could quibble, he was loading her plate.

It looked and smelt delicious and, somewhat to her surprise, she found she had a healthy appetite.

They ate in silence and when their plates were empty he put them in the dishwasher and poured coffee for them both.

Feeling tense, ill at ease, and dreading any further questioning, she gazed into the fire, wishing she was anywhere but where she was.

Resuming his seat, he looked at her steadily until the force of his will made her return his gaze.

When she lifted her eyes to his he said, 'Now, tell me what made you leave like you did, without a word.'

'I've already told you.'

'But not the full story. There has to be more to it than that. I want to know just *why* you decided to give up your job and go back to England?'

She shook her head mutely.

'As the person responsible for bringing you over here, don't you think I'm entitled to an explanation?'

When she remained stubbornly silent he attacked from another angle. 'If you were dead set on going, why didn't you ask me for whatever you needed? It was absolutely idiotic to leave like that, when you had no return ticket and no money.'

'How do you know I had no money?'

'When I talked to Richard he admitted that he'd loaned you enough to tide you over.'

'Then you were lying when you said Richard didn't give me away!'

'I wasn't, and he didn't. At first I had no idea that he'd even set eyes on you. It was from another source entirely that I got the first clue and learnt that Richard was involved in some way.

'He only came clean about the whole thing when I rang him up in Florida and told him that—' Daniel broke off abruptly.

'That you'd go down there and beat him up?'

He raised a dark brow.

'But then you're good at beating up lesser mortals, aren't you?' she went on bitterly.

His grey eyes alert and waiting, he asked, 'What makes you say that?'

Tension stretched between them, criss-crossed like fine, invisible wires.

'Just something I heard,' she mumbled. Adding quickly

before he could pursue the matter, 'I'm surprised you went to so much trouble to contact Richard. After all, there must be plenty of women who would be only too happy to keep your bed warm.'

Janice, for one.

A muscle jumped in his jaw before he observed coldly, 'All the mud the gutter press have thrown in the past seems to have stuck.'

She wanted to tell him she knew about Janice, and the way he'd lied. To throw Tim's death in his face. But, unable to, she said, 'I don't need what the papers have printed in the past to tell me what a complete and utter swine you are.'

'So what precisely are you accusing me of? If I don't know I can't begin to answer the charges.'

Watching her close up like an oyster he continued bleakly, 'Putting the past aside, I seem to be getting a bad press at the moment. Richard practically accused me of attacking you.'

She flushed. 'I'm sorry about that. It was quite unwarranted. I tried to tell him the whole thing had been my fault, but I found it difficult to explain why I'd left The Lilies so suddenly.'

He looked at her, a look that leapt between them live and burning. 'I just wish you could explain it to *my* satisfaction.'

When she failed to respond he said, 'At least tell me what I've done to make you call me a swine.'

'You forced me to come up here with you.'

'Surely there's more to it than that?'

'Isn't that enough?'

'If you'd been *really* set against coming you could have called my bluff.'

'I wish I had.'

Sighing, he gave up for the time being and rose. 'Well,

now you are here it would be a shame if you didn't see something of the countryside.'

Taking her hand, he pulled her to her feet. 'If you want to try a spot of snowmobiling go get your clothes on while I build up the fires and bring the Snowcat round.'

When she had wrapped up warmly Charlotte went out on the front porch where the air was as cold and intoxicating as chilled champagne.

Sun was shining from a cornflower-blue sky and the world was white and sparkling like icing on a wedding cake.

Drifting snow had formed bizarre shapes, creating dips and gullies and ridges with overhanging crests. It piled up against the veranda posts, coated the trunks of the trees and weighed down the green boughs of the giant spruce.

She was watching a big bird wheeling slowly overhead and casting a moving shadow on the snow when she heard the muted roar of an engine.

A few seconds later Daniel came round the side of the house riding a gleaming black machine that put her in mind of a powerful motorbike, except that it had runners instead of wheels.

Cutting the engine until the roar died to a purr, he drew up in a little flurry of loose snow. 'Have you ever ridden pillion on a motorbike?'

'Once or twice,' she admitted shortly.

Very much against her wishes, Tim had insisted on having a motorbike for his eighteenth birthday but, after a couple of minor accidents, afraid he'd kill himself, she had refused to keep up the payments and it had gone back.

'Well, you'll find the Snowcat a lot easier, more stable. Put this on—' he handed her a warmly lined helmet, similar to the one he was wearing '—and climb up behind.'

As soon as she was settled they set off, turning down the woodland track they had come along the previous night.

Sheltered by the windscreen and the bulk of his body it was nowhere near as cold as Charlotte had expected and, resolving to leave all her worries behind and live for the moment, she soon found she was enjoying herself.

After a while they picked up speed and the trees flashing past on either side added to the feeling of exhilaration.

'Liking it?' he asked over his shoulder.

'Loving it!' she answered enthusiastically.

For the next hour or so, skirting small hamlets and following various tracks and trails, they explored the surrounding countryside, stopping from time to time to take a look at various places of interest.

Having climbed gradually to the summit of a wooded hill, Daniel brought the Snowcat to a halt and said, 'Now, this is a view you mustn't miss.'

Leading her to a look-out point between the trees, he stood close behind her, his arms crossed over her breasts, his body shielding hers from the chill wind, and asked, 'Great, isn't it?'

'Wonderful,' she agreed.

He pointed a gloved finger. 'Over in that direction is Ashokan Reservoir and, further north, the village of Woodstock.'

As he moved his hand it brushed her breast and she shivered.

Feeling that involuntary movement he said, 'You're cold... We'd better get moving.'

By the time they had dropped down to an open, wind-scoured expanse that he told her was Beaver Lake, the sinking sun was laying long blue shadows on the golden snow and streaking the sky with pink and the palest of greens.

Skirting the lake, they followed a partly-frozen stream until they came to a rough log dam and, beyond, an ice-covered pond. What appeared to be a pile of small tree trunks and branches formed a flattish mound in the middle of the pond.

Bringing the Snowcat to a halt and cutting the engine he queried, 'Ever seen a beaver lodge at close quarters?'

'No... But I'd certainly like to.'

'Well, this might be your chance.'

Jumping down, he helped her off the machine and went to examine the pond.

'There's been quite a bit of activity here recently, which means the ice won't be too thick...'

Watching him, and listening to him, she realized she had always thought of him as a high-powered businessman, a city man through and through.

Now she was seeing him in a different light, hearing the echo of the boy who was familiar with these mountains; the boy who had hiked here in the summer and skied in the winter.

'But it should hold us if we move carefully, one at a time...'

Treading cautiously, he picked his way across the ice to stand on the mound, before turning to say drily, 'I wonder if this is where the phrase *walking on thin ice* originated?'

'It looks a bit dicey,' she agreed. 'I can see the water underneath in parts.'

'Still want to come?'

Knowing it might be the only chance she'd ever get, she said, 'Yes.'

'OK, go for it. Keep to the line I took, as near as you can.'

Without hesitation she began to cross, doing her best to follow the route he had taken. When she was close enough he reached out a hand and pulled her on to the mound beside him.

Looking at the pile of icy logs and branches that was supporting them, she asked, 'Is this *really* a beaver lodge?'

He smiled at the excitement in her voice before answering, 'It is indeed.'

'I can't see any way into it.'

'Though the beavers live above the water level the entrance to the lodge is always underwater.'

'How deep is the pond?'

'Say four feet, maybe a bit more,' he answered. Adding, with just a hint of mockery, 'Aren't you brave to have come across? Many a woman would have chickened out.'

Calmly, she told him, 'I figured that if the ice would stand your weight it would stand mine. You must be quite a bit heavier than I am.'

'Well, you should know,' he said wickedly.

Feeling her face suffuse with colour, she was turning hastily away when she slipped and lost her footing.

Reacting with lightning speed, Daniel caught her and held her close. Breathless and completely off balance, for a few seconds she lay against him, trying to gather herself.

Then, lifting her chin, she braced her hands against his chest to move away. Their eyes met and she glimpsed the naked desire in his.

As though moving in slow motion, he bent his head and, transfixed, she waited for his kiss. The instant their cold lips touched fire ran through her.

She remembered him saying, 'No one can plan the chemistry between two people. It has to be spontaneous combustion'.

Spontaneous combustion was what it was.

How long they stood there kissing, totally lost in each other, she never knew. The rest of the world and everything in it had ceased to exist the instant his mouth covered hers.

Daniel was the first to come to his senses and begin to draw back.

She hadn't wanted it to end and, feeling bereft, she opened dazed green eyes and gazed up at him.

He sighed. 'God knows I'd like nothing better than to go on kissing you…'

Her blood still coursing fast through her veins, she would have raised no objection if he'd wanted to make love to her there and then.

'But if we stay here much longer the amount of heat we're generating will melt the ice,' he added drily.

Seeing her look of regret, and misinterpreting it, he offered whimsically, 'If it'll make you feel any better you can lay the blame on me.'

Only too aware of her own uninhibited response, she shook her head.

'Well, don't start giving yourself hell.'

'I won't,' she said valiantly.

'That's my girl,' he approved. 'Now then, who's going first?'

Her legs still feeling shaky, and knowing she needed a bit longer to pull herself together, she said, 'You'd better.'

Watching him cross the ice in the gathering dusk Charlotte thought how lightly and gracefully he moved for so big a man. How superb he was physically.

How much she loved him.

While Daniel would never be the kind of man she wanted him to be, no other man would ever hold her heart like he did.

And, just for the moment, he was hers.

She found herself recalling her old school motto, *Carpe Diem*—Seize the day.

If she just let go of all the problems, tried to forget about Janice and the past, and simply enjoyed the here and now…

Reaching firm ground, he called, 'Come carefully.'

Her thoughts busy, she started to cross.

She was still some distance from the edge when he

warned sharply, 'You're moving off line. The ice is thinner there.'

Even as he spoke she heard the creak and felt it start to give beneath her feet.

CHAPTER NINE

'LIE down flat,' he ordered quietly. 'Spread your weight.'

Strangely calm, she lowered herself carefully.

'Now, give me your hands.'

She obeyed and, stretched full length on his stomach, Daniel reached out and caught both her gloved hands in his.

'Stay absolutely still.'

Digging in his toes, he inched backwards, dragging her to safety.

A second later he was up and helping her to her feet. 'All right?' he asked urgently.

Sensing that he was a lot more rattled than she was, she assured him, 'Right as rain.'

'I'm a blasted fool!' He denounced himself angrily. 'I should have been taking better care of you. If you'd gone in...'

'Even if I had, I'm hardly likely to have drowned.'

'But the water would have been damned cold,' he pointed out, his face serious, 'and if you're saturated shock and hypothermia can do an awful lot of damage.'

'Well, thanks to you, I'm suffering from neither. In fact, I'm bone dry and not even cold.'

As though to give lie to that last statement, she shivered involuntarily.

'Time we were heading back,' he said briskly. 'We're a fair distance from home and once it's dark it'll get even colder.'

As soon as she was settled behind him he switched on

the engine and, their lights making a bright tunnel through the gathering dusk, they headed back to the lodge.

While Daniel put the Snowcat away and built up the fires Charlotte made a pot of coffee and filled two mugs with the steaming liquid.

The instant she had walked into the lodge all the troubles, which earlier she'd tried to push on one side, had come crowding back. She knew that letting go would be impossible if she could neither forgive nor forget.

For the umpteenth time she went over the same ground. Though she loved him, Daniel Wolfe was not only a liar and a womanizer—it was his actions that had caused her brother's death.

But, as Carla was fond of pointing out, it takes two to tango and Janice must have been at least partly responsible.

Though, if Daniel had turned on the heat, the girl would have had about as much chance of not melting as a snowball in hell.

She knew that from bitter experience.

Take this afternoon, for instance. When she should have been trying to keep him at bay, the instant he had touched his lips to hers she had gone up in flames.

She had opened her mouth for him, met and matched his passion with a passion of her own, traded kiss for kiss.

If he'd wanted to lay her down and make love to her in a snowdrift she would have welcomed it.

She shivered, ashamed and humiliated by her own weakness, her lack of self-control and willpower.

In spite of Tim, in spite of Janice, in spite of knowing it would all end in tears, while she was with Daniel she was under his spell, her very soul held in bondage.

The sooner the holiday was over, the better. The only way she could be *sure* of not giving in to him would be to put an ocean between them...

But, even if she could persuade him to take her back to

New York tomorrow, she still had to get through the coming night. And how was she to do that without sinking any further in her own estimation?

It was a question to which she already knew the answer. If she was to keep any vestige of pride or self-respect, she must insist on Daniel sleeping on the couch.

But, when the crunch came, could she do it?

Yes, she could and *would*, she resolved…

When he joined her in front of the fire she felt taut as a drawn bow string and, as he sat down opposite, found herself avoiding his eyes.

'Something wrong?' he queried, picking up his coffee.

'What could possibly be wrong?' she asked sarcastically.

'I take it you still resent my being so…high-handed?'

'Don't you think I've every right to feel resentful? I didn't want to come here. I didn't want to sleep with you again… Oh, I know you didn't *make* me, but…' She tailed off unhappily.

Slowly, he said, 'So, despite all we shared last night, you'd sooner be sleeping alone in that damn brownstone?'

'Much sooner.'

Above the dark sweater his face looked hard and bleak. 'Well, if that's how you feel, we'll go back to town first thing tomorrow morning.'

Taking a deep breath, she told herself how relieved she was.

But she didn't *feel* relieved. If anything, she felt more miserable and mixed up than ever.

'In the meantime—' he went on, a hint of silky menace in his voice '—it's high time we stopped playing games and—'

'You're the only one who's playing games!' she burst out.

'I don't think so.'

Suddenly scared stiff, she whispered, 'What makes you say that?'

His grey eyes cold as steel, he told her, 'I'll ask the questions. And this time I intend to have some satisfactory answers.'

'Even if you have to beat them out of me...? Well, go ahead, you're a big brave man.'

Unmoved by her taunt, he said calmly, 'That won't be necessary. There are other ways.'

All at once the conversation had turned into a confrontation and, badly shaken, she took a gulp of her coffee and waited.

He let her wait.

As the seconds stretched she struggled to hold on to a spurious air of calm.

His first question, when it came, was quiet, almost casual. 'Tell me, Charlotte, why did you apply for the New York job?'

The question took her by surprise. Expecting him to ask again why she had left The Lilies so abruptly, she had been trying to think of an answer he would believe. Or, at the very least, accept.

Now she swallowed and said lamely, 'I needed a change...' Then, rallying, 'And I'd always wanted to see New York.'

'You must have wanted to quite badly, to have agreed to come at such short notice.'

'There was nothing to keep me in London.'

'So why the hurry to get back there?'

'I realized that it had been a bad mistake to come.'

'How could you be so sure, without even starting your new job?'

'It had nothing to do with the job. As I said before, it was a personal thing. I didn't intend to get mixed up with a man like you.'

'That wasn't my impression. In fact, I thought quite the opposite. At times you seemed more than happy to...shall we say...*encourage* me.'

'But I never meant to...' Realizing she was speaking the thought aloud, she broke off, flustered.

'You never meant to what? Actually sleep with me?'

Her flaming cheeks were answer enough.

'So what did you mean to do? Lead me on and then keep me dangling until I asked you to marry me?'

'Certainly not.'

'You wouldn't be the first woman to have tried it.'

An iron band tightening around her chest, she said sharply, 'Believe me, you're the last man in the world I'd want to marry.'

He cocked a dark brow at her. 'I can't imagine you've any serious reservations about having a wealthy husband and a comfortable lifestyle?'

'*If* I ever get married I'll need to trust my husband. No one in their right mind would trust a man with a reputation like yours.'

Driving home her point, she emphasized, 'As I've told you on more than one occasion I had no intention whatsoever of getting involved.'

'That's what you've *told* me,' he agreed. 'The trouble is, I didn't believe you then, and I don't believe you now.

'Despite my "reputation", from our very first meeting you showed every sign of wanting to attract me...'

She felt physically sick. Had it been so obvious?

'The night I took you to La Havane, you can't deny you set out to flirt with me, and later when I saw you up to your room—'

'I'd had too much to drink.' she broke in jerkily.

'Having too much to drink can be to blame for a lot of things, but it doesn't make you kiss a man you seriously don't want to get involved with.'

'I hate you!' she burst out furiously.

Looking unmoved, he said, 'I believe I know you well enough by now to be sure that if you hated me you wouldn't have gone to bed with me.'

'I *do* hate you,' she choked, seeing again Janice's pretty, startled face.

Shaking his head, he disagreed quietly, 'You may *want* to hate me, but I don't think you do, in spite of what happened to your stepbrother.'

There was complete and utter silence. The rustle of a log settling, the whisper of falling ash, the ticking of the clock the only sounds.

'So you weren't aware I knew? Thinking about it,' he added slowly, 'that makes sense.'

Her voice sounding strange in her own ears, she asked, 'How long have you known Tim was my stepbrother?'

'I've always known.'

'How did you find out?'

'Telford told me. He warned me that you had been very upset and angry over my part in what had happened...

'Which made me wonder just why you'd applied for, and accepted, the New York job when it was bound to bring us closer together.'

Finding it difficult to breathe, she sat quite still, her eyes on his face.

'So why did you, Charlotte? Were you hoping to exact payment? Get some kind of revenge?'

When she failed to deny it he asked, a shade mockingly, 'What had you in mind? Not a knife in the ribs, obviously...

'Let me see. At a guess, I'd say you were hoping to make me fall for you without getting too involved yourself. And certainly without sleeping with me,' he added wryly. 'Then, when I was well and truly hooked, emotionally as well as physically, throw a bombshell in my face.'

'Have I guessed right? Yes, I can see by your expression that I have. So what went wrong? Why did you run as you did?'

It took a moment or two to find her voice. When she did, she lied desperately, 'Nothing went wrong. I—I just realized that I couldn't go through with it after all.'

'Why couldn't you go through with it?'

When she remained silent he persisted. 'If you still wanted revenge for my part in your stepbrother's death, I don't understand why—'

Needing to distract him, she broke in, 'What *I* don't understand is, if you knew Tim was my stepbrother, why didn't you mention it sooner?'

'I was waiting for *you* to bring things into the open, so I could answer any charges, but though I gave you every opportunity you never said a word.

'At first I hoped you might have decided to put the whole thing behind you and let bygones be bygones. Or, at the very least, have come to see what happened in a more rational light.

'However, it soon became evident that you were still angry, that you still thought I was largely to blame for your stepbrother's death.'

'You're quite wrong,' she said, and saw his little blink of surprise before she went on trenchantly, 'I think you're *entirely* to blame.

'You seduced his fiancée and, when he faced you with it, you beat him up and fired him before having him thrown out. If it hadn't been for you he'd still be alive.

'Now, answer those charges if you can!'

'I can,' Daniel said with quiet conviction.

His face was like granite and, when his eyes met hers, she saw that their usual silvery colour had darkened almost to charcoal, swallowing the pupils.

'I'll answer the dismissal accusation first, because it's the only one that's just. Yes, I sacked him. In the circumstances I couldn't do anything else—'

'Of course you couldn't! How could you possibly go on employing a man whose fiancée you were bedding?'

'I was doing nothing of the kind.'

'Are you trying to tell me it was just a one-night stand?'

'Not even that,' he said unhesitatingly.

Jumping to her feet, she faced him furiously, 'I don't want any of your lies or excuses.'

'You won't get any.' His voice had an edge like a steel blade as he went on, 'All you'll get from me is the truth. If you want to hear it, I suggest you sit down and listen.'

Subsiding into her chair, she bit her lip.

'The afternoon it all began, Mrs Weldon, the secretary I usually use when I'm in London, had an urgent dental appointment…'

Charlotte knew Mrs Weldon, a middle-aged dragon of a woman with a sharp manner and an even sharper tongue, who kept the younger secretaries firmly in their place.

'So a Miss Jeffries, whom I'd never set eyes on before, was sent to fill in. She was quick and efficient but, as Telford was at a three-day conference in Paris there was a lot of work to get through, and it was almost six-thirty by the time we'd finished.

'I thanked her for staying late, promised she'd be paid overtime, and said goodnight. She went back to her own office and, as far as I was concerned, that was that.

'Though earlier in the day the weather had been pleasant and sunny, by late afternoon it had started to rain heavily. I had no coat, so I rang for a taxi to take me back to my hotel.

'As I crossed the lobby I noticed Miss Jeffries was just ahead of me. She was wearing a light jacket and had no umbrella. My taxi was just drawing up outside, so I offered her a lift.

'She hesitated for a second or two, then thanked me and got in. I asked her where she lived and she told me St Elphin Street, but said quickly that she didn't want to go straight home.

'After a moment, sounding uptight, she went on to say that she was planning to get something to eat and perhaps see a show, so could I drop her off somewhere near Charing Cross Road, if that wasn't out of my way?

'I assured her that it wasn't. Then, seeing that she still looked tense and nervous, I asked her if everything was all right.

'She said yes, fine, and promptly burst into tears. I passed her a handkerchief and waited.

'When we got to Charing Cross Road she was still crying and it was raining harder than ever. My hotel was on the Strand and, acting on the spur of the moment, I invited her to have dinner with me—'

'Do you usually invite other men's fiancées out to dinner?' Charlotte broke in curtly.

'At that point I had no idea she was engaged and she looked so young and vulnerable—'

'Janice may have looked young and vulnerable, but she wore an engagement ring.'

'She wasn't wearing one that day.'

'She always wore it,' Charlotte insisted, recalling how proud the girl had been of the modest solitaire that—with Charlotte's help—Tim had bought her.

'Both her hands were bare,' Daniel said flatly.

When Charlotte relapsed into silence, speaking evenly, dispassionately, he continued, 'To cut a long story short, Miss Jeffries accepted my invitation and, while we ate, she poured out all her troubles.

'First of all she told me that she and her boyfriend had had a terrific bust up and she had given him back his ring—'

'You're lying!' Charlotte cried furiously. 'When I went on holiday just a few days before they both appeared perfectly happy and were planning a September wedding.'

'I don't doubt it. In fact, what Miss Jeffries said confirmed it. But she also told me, without being specific, that "something had happened" to throw those plans into turmoil and threaten the whole relationship.

'Which, at the time, made me wonder if her boyfriend had been—how shall I put it?—playing away from home.'

'How dare you suggest such a thing? Not all men are rotten through and through, like you.'

Daniel's strong mouth tightened before he said patiently, 'Well, he was a man and it does happen.'

'Not in their case,' she denied vehemently. 'Tim absolutely adored Janice. He wouldn't have willingly done anything to jeopardise the relationship.'

'You said *willingly*, and I'm sure you're right... But what if it was something he couldn't help?'

'I don't know what you mean.'

'Well, I suggest we go into that later. In the meantime I'll carry on, if you'll allow me to.'

Biting her lip, Charlotte waited.

After a moment he resumed. 'Miss Jeffries went on to say she was starting to think that moving in together and getting engaged had been a terrible mistake. But, in the circumstances, she was afraid if she told him that it would only make things worse.

'With no idea of the circumstances, at that stage I could offer no advice. All I could do was listen.

'When the meal was over we had coffee in the lounge and at that point she seemed a little more cheerful. But at nine-thirty, when I suggested calling a taxi to take her home, she burst into tears again and said she couldn't face going back to the flat; she needed more time to think.

'Realizing I was stuck with the wretched girl, I booked her a single room, saw her up to it, and left her at her door.'

Seeing Charlotte's expression, he added firmly, 'I never laid so much as a finger on her.'

'I bet!' she muttered.

A muscle jumped spasmodically in his jaw before he went on evenly, 'The following morning we ate breakfast together, then I sent her home in a taxi while I walked to the office.

'An hour or so later I was standing by the window dictating some letters to Mrs Weldon when the door burst open. A strange young man rushed in and—'

'And you knocked him down.'

'Yes, I knocked him down—'

'You must have been pleased with yourself.'

Ignoring the jibe, Daniel went on, 'But only after he'd floored me first.'

'A big strong man like you?' she taunted.

'If I remember correctly, he was as tall as I am and a good few pounds heavier.'

'He was only a boy.'

'The "boy",' as you call him, took me by surprise and, before I realized what was going on, I was flat on my back and he was putting the boot in—'

'I don't believe it.'

'It's the truth. Your accusation that I "beat him up" wasn't justified, Charlotte. Everything I did was done in self-defence.

'If you don't want to take my word you can check with Mrs Weldon and the hospital where, later, I had to have a couple of cracked ribs strapped up.'

Ignoring her horrified face, his voice even, he continued, 'When I found out who he was and what was bugging him I told him the exact truth about what had happened.

'He told me to go to hell and made it clear that he didn't

believe either his fiancée or me. He was creating such a disturbance that I was forced to have him escorted from the building.'

'You mean have him thrown out.'

'Call it what you will.'

'And you didn't feel a moment's guilt for the part you'd played?'

'No, I didn't. But I did feel some degree of sympathy for him when I realized how it must have *appeared*, and I was sorry to have inadvertently sparked the whole thing off.

'So, before I started for the airport that afternoon, I left a message for Telford explaining briefly what had happened and telling him to give your stepbrother time to cool off and then offer him his job back.

'As far as I was concerned that was the end of the matter and, apart from some bodily discomfort, I scarcely gave it another thought.

'Then I heard the tragic news that your stepbrother had died from a lethal cocktail of drink and drugs whilst trying to drown his sorrows.'

'And you still felt no guilt?'

'I felt partly to blame,' he said quietly. 'That's why I got in touch with Miss Jeffries and went over for the funeral service.'

She hadn't known that. Somehow the press must have missed it. Which seemed strange.

As though reading her thoughts he said, 'Dodging the press wasn't easy.'

Curiously she asked, 'How did you manage it?'

'I didn't want to add any more fuel to the fire, so I arrived at the church very early and the vicar gave me the use of a private room. After the service I went back there until everyone else had gone home and the press had dispersed.

'That evening I had a long talk with Miss Jeffries. Naturally she was very upset and blamed herself for what had happened. She kept saying, "I wish I'd tackled the problem differently. I wish I'd stayed at home that night"...'

'I wish she had,' Charlotte said. 'Tim would have still been alive if you and she hadn't—' A lump in her throat, she stopped speaking abruptly.

'So you still think I'm lying?'

'What else can I think?'

'You could try believing me.'

'I *might* have believed you if you hadn't brought her over here so you could carry on your affair...'

As he began to shake his head she cried, 'I know she's in New York. I saw her with my own eyes, so don't attempt to deny it.'

'I've no intention of denying it. In fact, quite the opposite. But you're wrong in thinking she's here because we're having an affair.'

She *wanted* to believe him, but couldn't.

'Richard told me that *you'd* had her transferred over here. Why else would you have done that?'

'I offered her a job in New York, a change of scene, when she discovered she couldn't stay where she was and handed in her notice.'

'Why couldn't she stay where she was?'

'Some of the London staff believed the allegations in the press and made things very difficult for her.'

'Surely that wasn't your concern?'

'As I'd been involved, however innocently, I felt it was. Luckily, however, the move seems to have worked out well—'

'I'm sure it has,' Charlotte broke in bitterly. 'In fact, it seems to have "worked out well" for everybody but poor Tim.'

'I agree that your stepbrother was a victim, but he was a victim of circumstance, of his own weakness, rather than—'

Her hands clenched into fists of rage, she jumped to her feet and, her voice rising shrilly, cried, 'Don't you dare criticize Tim! If it hadn't been for you and that little—' Covering her face with her hands, she burst into tears.

When Daniel moved to take her in his arms she tried to fight him off. 'Leave me alone, damn you.'

Despite her struggles, he gathered her close and, sitting down, pulled her on to his lap.

After Tim's death she had somehow kept moving through the shock and trauma, through the pain and futile anger, but she had never really wept for him.

Now she did, the sorrow and grief seeping from her like blood from an open wound.

Cradling her head against his shoulder, Daniel let her cry for a while before he said quietly, 'I know you loved your stepbrother and coming back to find him dead, as you did, must have been a terrible blow. Naturally, you want someone to blame, but—'

'I blame myself,' she sobbed. 'If I'd been there to take care of him…'

'Don't be foolish.' Daniel's voice was gentle but his words packed a punch. 'Tim wasn't a child; he was a grown man. Almost twenty-two. Old enough to take care of himself. Old enough to be responsible for his own actions.

'You can't blame yourself. With hindsight, we all might *wish* we'd done things differently. But what's done can't be undone, and it shouldn't be allowed to darken the future with vain regrets and futile guilt.'

Handing her a folded handkerchief, he urged, 'Come on now, dry your eyes.'

As, her emotions still in turmoil, she scrambled off his lap and scrubbed at her face, he added matter-of-factly, 'It's about time we had something to eat. After an afternoon spent in the open air you must be getting hungry. I know I am.'

Needing time alone to sort her thoughts into some kind of order, she gathered herself and asked, 'Would you like me to cook a meal?'

Rising to his feet, he shook his head. 'As soon as you're ready I'm taking you over to Marchais for dinner. We have a table reserved for seven-thirty or thereabouts.'

Surprised, she asked thickly, 'On Christmas Day? I didn't realize any restaurants would be open.'

'Where we're going is no ordinary restaurant. It's a hotel, part of a holiday complex.

'Though they will no doubt be serving a traditional Christmas menu tonight, the cooking is usually first class and there'll be music and dancing and a real party atmosphere.'

Mixed-up and depressed, and with an incipient headache, she had never felt less like venturing into a party atmosphere.

'If you don't mind, I'd rather not go.'

Firmly he said, 'I do mind. In my opinion it'll do you good to get out.'

The last thing she wanted in her present mood was to 'be done good to' she thought rebelliously.

'Now, go and get ready, there's a good girl.'

The deliberately patronising last few words told her he was trying to rile her. Hadn't he once remarked that anger was easier to deal with than depression?

Deciding that his strategy wasn't going to work, she said jerkily, 'I'm rather tired, not particularly hungry and I've got the beginnings of a headache.'

He disappeared into the kitchen to return after a moment with two small white tablets and a glass of water. 'Take these. They should get rid of your headache quite quickly.'

When she had obediently swallowed them, a gleam in his eye, he threw down the gauntlet. 'If you find you *still* want to stay in we can always share a can of soup and have a nice early night.'

A shiver ran through her.

Perhaps, until she'd sorted out her thoughts and feelings, a party atmosphere and being amongst people would be preferable to staying here alone with Daniel.

Still not totally sure if she could trust herself, despite her resolve, common sense told her it would certainly be *safer*. Her emotions weren't completely under control and, if they surfaced once more, she might well find she was only too susceptible to the comfort he would almost certainly offer.

Watching her expressive face, he grinned suddenly and asked, 'Do I win? Or do I win?'

'You win,' she conceded. And, her heart turning over at that unexpected smile, added, 'If you dare be seen out with me. I must look a fright.'

Using a single finger he tilted her chin and studied her swollen eyes and blotched face. 'Don't worry, my love. Though you look a little woebegone, there's nothing a splash of cold water won't cure.'

Just for a second that 'my love' rocked her and she thought passionately, if only things were different, if only she *was* his love.

But casual endearments like that were no doubt easy coin, part of his stock-in-trade. Daniel had no time for love or commitment; the only genuine emotion he felt, the driving force of his life, was lust.

She stepped back abruptly and his hand dropped to his side.

He looked about to speak and, oddly afraid of what he might say, she turned and fled.

After bathing her puffy eyes and splashing her cheeks

with cold water she took a hot shower, which made her feel a great deal better.

Then, determined to put a brave face on it, she dressed in the midnight-blue cocktail dress she had worn the night he took her to La Havane, coiled her red-gold hair into a sleek chignon, and made-up with care.

Court shoes on her feet, she was about to pull on her cloak when a thought struck her and she paused. Daniel hadn't said how they were going to get to Marchais. She might have to change into something more suitable for travelling on the back of a snowmobile.

Her cloak over her arm, she went through to the living-room where the fire had been banked up and the guard placed in front of it.

There was no sign of Daniel, but at that instant the front door opened and he came in wearing a short car coat.

'All ready, I see. And looking especially lovely.' His voice was husky and the glow in his eyes seemed to scorch her skin.

She found herself stammering, 'I—I wasn't sure what I should be wearing. How we were getting there...'

'This will do fine.' Taking the cloak, he moved behind her.

As he placed it around her shoulders she felt his momentary hesitation, the warmth of his breath on her neck, and waited with bated breath for his lips to touch her nape.

Instead, he stepped back, saying levelly, 'Marchais is less than a mile and, had it been summer, we could easily have walked. As it is, the car seemed the most sensible option.'

Apart from the tension between them, which was wholly sexual, there was an air of do or die about him, a sense of purpose, as though he was preparing himself for his own personal Armageddon.

CHAPTER TEN

OUTSIDE, the four wheel drive was waiting by the porch, its engine ticking over smoothly.

It was a star-pricked night, cold and clear, except for a single cloud formation stretching like a range of snowy mountains. As she watched, an almost full moon sailed into view, a long thin wisp of cloud trailing from it. It put her in mind of a silver helium-filled balloon.

The empty moonwashed snowscape seemed eerily still until an errant breeze stirred the green arms of the pine and blew snow like white mist.

When they were settled in the warmth of the car Daniel drove to the road and set off carefully down the hill. After a hundred yards or so he turned into a side road, little more than a wide track through the woods.

Charlotte saw lights gleaming and, a second or two later, they drove through an archway into a well-lit parking-area with buildings on all sides.

It was hung with strings of coloured lights and a pair of tall glistening Christmas trees flanked a short flight of steps up to the hotel.

There were quite a lot of vehicles already parked but Daniel found a vacant space near the steps and eased the car into it.

As soon as they left the car they could hear the sound of music. At the top of the steps double doors opened into a carpeted lobby with a cloakroom on one side and a blazing log fire on the other.

Daniel lifted Charlotte's cloak from her shoulders and

deposited that and his own coat before they made their way through to a lavishly decorated restaurant.

At first glance all the tables scattered around a polished dance floor seemed to be occupied and, mingling with the music made by a small group, there was a buzz of talk and laughter.

As they reached the archway a pleasant-looking man somewhere in his early fifties appeared and greeted them. 'Mr Wolfe…Miss Michaels…I'm so glad you could make it.'

'Bill, how are you?' The two men shook hands.

'Fine, thanks. Keeping busy.'

'And the rest of the family?'

'All well except Kate's mother, who's confined to bed after a fall… You know the young ones are up for Christmas? They're visiting over at Dalen End at the moment but asked me to say they'll have a word when they get back.

'Gordon's here too. When he leaves college next year he's decided to stay on and help us run the place, which is good news…'

Still talking, he led them to a table set at a discreet distance both from the neighbouring tables and the dance floor.

'How does this suit you? If you prefer, I can have you moved closer to the action?'

'No, this is ideal, thanks,' Daniel assured him.

When they were both seated, Bill lowered his voice and said, 'I'm well aware that Christmas Day isn't the time to talk business, but this afternoon I heard an interesting whisper with regard to that piece of real estate we were discussing last month… So, if you can spare just a minute before you go…?'

Turning to Charlotte, Daniel asked politely, 'If my guest has no objections?'

'No, of course not,' she answered immediately.

'Then I'll come along to your office later,' Daniel told him.

'Thanks. Enjoy your meal, now.' Looking relieved, he hurried away.

'Sorry about that,' Daniel said. 'But Bill has been waiting for an adjacent property to come on the market. He has plans to extend Marchais, and I've agreed in principle to provide the additional financial backing needed.'

A waiter appeared at Daniel's elbow with a plate of hors-d'oeuvre and a wine list.

Daniel consulted Charlotte. 'As we'll no doubt be having goose, I suggest a good claret... Unless you'd sooner have champagne?'

Determined to stay stone cold sober, she said, 'You have whatever you like. I really don't want any wine, thank you. I'd prefer sparkling water.'

With a nod to the waiter, Daniel said, 'As I'm driving, we'll both stick with sparkling water.'

When the man had moved away, Daniel queried solicitously, 'Do you still have a headache?'

Without thinking, she admitted, 'No, it's gone.'

His smile sardonic, he said, 'I see... So you're just being cautious.'

Drat the man! Charlotte thought vexedly. He could read her like a book.

Rising, he offered her his hand. 'As your headache's gone, perhaps you'd care to dance?'

Afraid that being held in his arms might undermine her resolve, she was about to refuse when, realizing it might be the last chance she would ever get, she found herself saying, 'Yes, I'd like to.'

As they threaded their way through the tables, the group changed from ballroom music to a disco number. To her surprise, instead of backing off, he drew her on to the floor and began to move easily to the rhythm.

Missing the thing she'd been afraid of, and scared he'd notice her disappointment, she remarked lightly, 'Neat footwork.'

Smiling mockingly, he asked, 'Did you imagine I couldn't disco at my great age?'

Flustered, she said, 'Of course not. It's just that somehow I'd expected your taste in dancing to be more...sophisticated.'

'I admit that I usually prefer to hold my partner... But now, watching the way you move your hips, I'm starting to see what I've been missing.'

Her colour rising, she looked away and tried to concentrate on the beat.

After dancing to another couple of numbers, they returned to their table. He had seated her and was moving to sit opposite when Charlotte noticed him glance up and, as though he had seen someone he knew, incline his head.

At that instant, their food arrived.

The Christmas fare of goose followed by plum pudding and brandy sauce proved to be excellent. But Daniel ate sparingly, said little, and had an air of tension, of *waiting*, that made Charlotte feel edgy.

She wondered just how important his business was.

Very important, apparently, as, the moment he had finished his coffee, he poured her a second cup and politely excused himself.

He had been gone only a moment or two when she caught a glimpse of a young woman, blonde and pretty, making for her table.

A woman she knew only too well.

So this was what had caused Daniel's tension, what he'd been waiting for.

Chin held high, her cheeks bearing a hectic flush, Janice

said, 'I hope you don't mind me coming over like this, but I—'

'I'm afraid you've just missed Daniel,' Charlotte informed her coldly.

The girl shook her head. 'He thought it would be better if I talked to you alone. May I sit down?'

When, battling with her chaotic thoughts, Charlotte failed to answer, Janice dropped into the chair Daniel had vacated and said quickly, 'Please listen to what I have to say...'

Looking desperately young and anxious she went on, 'I know you're not going to like what I have to tell you, but I—'

'You needn't tell me anything. I already know.'

'You do? Tim said he'd managed to keep it from you and, for some reason, possibly because they were focused on Mr Wolfe's involvement, the press didn't dig it out—'

'Dig what out?' Charlotte asked abruptly.

'That Tim was on drugs.'

All the colour draining from her face, Charlotte said sharply, 'I don't believe you. I know when he got in with that wild crowd at college he drank a bit but he always swore he steered clear of drugs.'

'That's what he told me when we moved in together. But it wasn't true. The combination of drink and drugs that killed him wasn't just a one-off, ''drowning his sorrows'', as everyone believed.

'He'd had a close call on more than one occasion. The first time I found him unconscious I was horrified. I was about to call the hospital when he came round and stopped me. That was when he admitted he was on drugs...'

'Oh, dear God,' Charlotte whispered.

'He swore he could keep it under control but once he was out with the crowd and drinking heavily he seemed to lose all sense of caution...

'Each time he promised he'd stop, kick the habit. I

begged him to get help but he said he didn't need outside help, he could manage it alone. All he had to do was stop drinking.

'But he didn't even try. He still kept on going out with those so-called friends…

'Then one morning, the morning it all started, I got up to find him slumped in the bathroom, too hungover to go to work. I told him I had no intention of staying around to watch him kill himself and gave him back his ring.

'That night when I left work it was raining heavily and Mr Wolfe offered me a lift. He asked me what was wrong and I'm afraid I broke down and cried in the taxi. He took me back to his hotel and bought me dinner.

'I told him I'd ended my engagement, but I didn't tell him *why*. I was afraid that if he knew Tim was on drugs he'd fire him…

'When it was time to go home, I just couldn't face it. Though he probably wondered what he'd done to be landed with a half-hysterical employee, he was kindness itself. He booked me a single room and told me to try and get a good night's sleep.

'In the morning he insisted on me eating some breakfast—I'd been too upset to eat much the previous night—then he sent me home in a taxi.

'When Tim asked me where I'd been all night I told him exactly what had happened, but he wouldn't believe me. He said he understood now why I'd given him back his ring, that I'd got bigger fish to fry.

'I told him not to be ridiculous. It had all been completely innocent—'

'And was it?'

'Of course it was…'

There was no mistaking the ring of truth in the girl's answer.

'I can't imagine how anyone could believe for an instant

that a man like Mr Wolfe, who could have his pick of beautiful women, would bother with the likes of me.'

'The press certainly thought so.'

'It was the scene Tim created at the office that made them think that. Of course the fight wouldn't have been news in the first place if Mr Wolfe hadn't been involved.

'It's difficult to keep a thing like that quiet and, as soon as they got wind of it, they were after him like a pack of wolves.

'But, though they must have made his life a misery, he still came over for the funeral. I thought that was very good of him. He didn't *have* to risk getting in any deeper.

'Later we had a really long talk. I told him everything, all about Tim's drug-taking and how bitterly sorry I was that, though I'd loved him, I'd been unable to help him.'

She swallowed hard. 'I'm sorry. I know you must blame me for his death. I'll never cease to regret that I walked out like I did, but I was at the end of my tether....

'I've often wished I'd been brave enough to tell *you* what was going on, but Tim was so adamant that you shouldn't know... You might have been able to save him.'

Giving the comfort that was needed, Charlotte admitted sadly, 'I very much doubt it. If the woman he loved and wanted to marry couldn't do it, I think the only one who could possibly have saved him was himself.'

Janice sighed. 'For a long time I blamed myself. I still do in a lot of ways... Though I mustn't let Martin hear me say that. I promised I'd do my best to put the past behind me.'

'Do you think you can?'

'I'm not sure. Talking to you might have helped. At least it's one thing off my mind. I just wish I'd had the courage to do it before. But I felt sure you'd blame me, and I couldn't take any more. All I wanted to do was get right

away from the whole sorry mess. That's why, when Mr
Wolfe offered me a transfer to New York, I took it.'

'I gather from a remark Daniel made earlier that things
have worked out well?'

Janice hesitated, then said in a rush, 'I don't know how
you're going to feel about this, but Martin and I liked the
look of each other on sight, and we've just got engaged…'

So Daniel *had* been speaking the truth. Charlotte felt
almost dizzy with relief. Aloud, she said, 'Martin? Martin
Shawcross?'

'Yes.'

All the separate pieces fell into place.

'His parents own Marchais and—' Janice stopped speaking as Daniel and a short fair-haired man approached the
table.

His eyes fixed on Charlotte's face, Daniel asked, 'All
right?'

Gathering herself, she answered evenly, 'Yes, thank you,
quite all right.'

Drawing the younger man forward, Daniel said, 'Charlotte, may I introduce Martin Shawcross… Martin, this is
Charlotte Michaels.'

Charlotte held out her hand. 'How do you do?'

Martin, who had a chubby face and amber eyes and
looked as good-natured as a teddy bear, shook her hand
and said with determined cheerfulness, 'Nice to meet you
at last, Miss Michaels.'

'It was good of you to let me borrow your flat.'

'I hope your stay there wasn't too uncomfortable?'

'No, not at all,' she lied.

'Won't you join us?' Daniel invited.

After a quick, interrogative glance at Janice, which she
answered with a slight smile, he said, 'Thanks, we'd love
to.'

As Daniel signalled a waiter to bring another couple of

chairs, Martin queried, 'I presume you've already had your meal?'

At Daniel's nod he went on, 'We ate at my grand-mother's. She would have been here but, unfortunately, she's confined to bed after a fall, so we went over to Dalen End to tell her the good news.'

Looking warily at Charlotte, as though fearing her re-action, he put an arm around Janice and said firmly, 'We've just got engaged.'

'Yes, I know. Janice told me. I'm very pleased for you both.'

His face showed his transparent relief.

'This calls for champagne,' Daniel said, his voice echo-ing that relief.

An ice-bucket containing a bottle of Bollinger and four champagne flutes appeared as if by magic. The waiter had eased out the cork with a satisfying pop and poured three glasses when Daniel stopped him and, indicating just a mouthful in the fourth, explained to Janice and Martin, 'I'm driving.'

'Why don't you leave the car here and let Gordon, my younger brother, take you home in the sleigh?' Martin sug-gested. 'He'll be ferrying quite a few of the local people later, so it will be there waiting.'

'I can always pick up the car in the morning if you fancy a sleigh-ride back?' Daniel raised an eyebrow at Charlotte.

'Sounds lovely,' she agreed.

For the next hour, while they drank champagne and danced, refusing to think about what she had learnt, she simply enjoyed the evening.

At ten-thirty, Daniel excused them on the grounds that they were travelling back to New York the following morn-ing and would need to make a fairly early start.

When he had collected their coats they said their good-nights and climbed into the waiting sleigh. Gordon clicked to the horse and a moment later they were being waved off by the entire family.

The light from twin lanterns gleaming golden on the snow, the muffled clip-clop of the horse's hooves and the jingle of the sleigh bells made the short ride back through the moonlit night spellbinding.

If Daniel had put his arm around her Charlotte's cup would have been running over but, making no move to touch her, he sat quietly, leaving six inches of space between them.

A large white owl, beautiful and ghost-like, swooped silently across in front of them and disappeared into the trees.

She glanced at Daniel, expecting his face to reflect something of the awe and pleasure she had felt at the sight.

But, though he must have seen it, his expression was serious and preoccupied, as though he had more important things on his mind.

She wondered if he was angry that she hadn't believed him when he'd told her the truth about himself and Janice earlier that evening.

When they reached Hailstone Lodge he jumped out and handed her down. Then, standing together on the porch, they thanked Gordon, answered his cheerful 'Good night,' and watched him drive away.

Having ushered her inside, Daniel took her cloak and hung that and his coat up, before joining her in front of the fire.

Though she had deliberately chosen the couch, hoping he would sit beside her, he moved to a chair.

Her heart sank.

After a moment he broke the silence to say, 'I'm afraid it's been a tough night for you.'

'You arranged for Janice to talk to me.'

'As we were so close it seemed to be the ideal opportunity. I didn't see how you could go on not knowing the truth about Tim's drug habit.'

'I should have known sooner… Should have guessed…'

'Why should you? He kept it pretty quiet. Even the press didn't pick it up. Presumably Miss Jeffries wouldn't have found out if they hadn't decided to live together.'

Charlotte sighed. 'I wish I had known. There might have been *something* I could have done.'

'I doubt it,' Daniel said quietly. 'I think he would have kept making the same empty promises to you as he made to Miss Jeffries.'

'You're probably right. It must have been hard.'

'Then you no longer blame her?'

'No. I think she did the best she could. To have done any more she would have needed Tim's cooperation.'

'And you're happy that there isn't and never was anything between us?'

'Yes. I owe you an apology.'

He shook his head. 'I can't blame you for thinking what you did. When I refused to cooperate with the press they went to town.

'It was Miss Jeffries I felt sorry for. She really loved your stepbrother.'

'Love doesn't solve everything.'

'So you said once before. Tell me about your engagement. What caused the break up?'

Surprised by the change of direction, she said, 'After a time I realized I'd agreed to marry Peter for all the wrong reasons.'

When she failed to elaborate, rather than ask what those reasons were, Daniel queried, 'What kind of man was he?'

'An unhappy one. He'd spent most of his childhood in boarding schools. A birth defect had left him with a leg he dragged slightly, which made him the butt of unkind jokes.'

'How did you get to know him?'

'I met him at an art class and liked him on sight. He was fair-haired and extremely handsome, with a sweet smile. At first he appeared shy, diffident, only too aware of his slight disability.

'We had coffee together and he told me that his girlfriend had walked out on him…'

At first, a supplicant at her feet, he had appeared dazzled by her, almost embarrassingly grateful for her slightest attention.

There had been an appealing 'little boy lost' air about him but, after a while, her beauty an obvious morale booster, he had gone from strength to strength, looking happier, gaining confidence.

'After a few weeks I agreed to have dinner with him. He took me to Longfellows…'

'In order to show you off, no doubt,' Daniel said. Adding drily, 'But who could blame him?'

'Peter was good company and we got on well together, discovering quite a lot in common. Apart from his art, which he was passionate about, he seemed gentle and unassuming…'

She had been delighted that there had been none of the macho pressure that, feeling threatened by it, she had come to hate.

'But, as soon as we got engaged, everything changed. Overnight almost, he became terribly demanding…'

Not only had he pressured her to sleep with him, but his constant complaints and demands had worn her out and frayed her nerves. He had wanted her by his side all the time and begrudged every moment he hadn't got her sole attention.

On the rare occasions they had gone out, if she so much as glanced at another man he had flown into a jealous rage. When, resenting the charge that she had flirted with a good-looking waiter, she had fought back, Peter had begun to play on his weakness, saying she didn't care about him because he was disabled.

'Knowing he must have been warped by his childhood, and pitying him, I tried to make allowances...'

And she had kept trying, much to Carla's disgust.

'For God's sake,' her friend had cried, "can't you see what he's doing to you? He doesn't love you; he only wants to use you. He's like a parasite.'

It had taken her a while to see the truth of Carla's words and even longer to cut herself free.

'In the end, almost suffocated by him, I gave him back his ring.'

'Never underestimate the strength of weakness,' Daniel said soberly. 'Especially when love's involved.'

'Though at the time I *thought* I was in love, with hindsight I realized I'd simply felt sorry for him.'

Rising to his feet, Daniel leaned against the mantel, his hands in his pockets, on his face a curious mixture of determination and resignation.

'Tell me, Charlotte, have you ever been *really* in love?'

Her heart seemed to stop. 'Why do you ask?'

'I'm curious.'

When she said nothing, he went on, 'You see, you still haven't told me why you left The Lilies so suddenly. Why you couldn't bring yourself to stay and go through with the revenge you'd been planning.

'You must have known that your scheme was working. It should have been easy...

'Unless you discovered that *you* were getting in too deep... And, because of who I am, you couldn't risk becoming emotionally involved...

'Was that it? You were in danger of falling in love with me?'

Somehow she pulled herself together and, putting as much scorn into her voice as she could muster, said, 'Do you seriously imagine that I'd be in danger of falling in love with a man who regards women merely as playthings?'

His voice cool, he asked, 'Apart from stories in the gutter press, what makes you think I regard women as play-things?'

'You told me yourself that you preferred sex on a "no-strings-involved, purely recreational basis"...'

'That isn't what—'

'And later in the conversation you said that as far as women were concerned you were "happy to keep things light"...'

She stopped speaking as, with one swift movement, he crossed to the couch and, taking her beneath the elbows, lifted her to her feet.

'If you think back you may recall that my remark was "*until now* I've been happy to keep things light"...'

Looking into her face, he said softly, 'But you're not the kind of woman to give yourself lightly, so why did you go to bed with me, Charlotte?'

'You must have heard of lust.'

'I've not only heard of it, I've experienced it many times. That's why I know the difference between love and lust. Love adds a whole load of extra dimensions.

'It also unlocks tongues,' he added cryptically. 'When I found out that you'd visited our offices—'

'How did you find out?'

'As luck would have it, when the financial meeting was over I bumped into Miss Jeffries. She was upset because she hadn't stopped to speak to you. Though she knew you were over in the States, seeing you waiting in the foyer took her by surprise.

'But, to get back to the point... Having checked with our receptionist, who had seen Richard take your suitcase, I went in search of him, only to find he'd already left for Florida.

'When I could find no trace of you at the apartment, or anywhere else, I assumed that you'd gone with him and I spent a sleepless night imagining the pair of you together.

'The next morning I did what I should have done in the first place, had I been in my right mind. I checked with the airline. I soon found he'd travelled alone and none of the Florida flights had carried a Miss Michaels.

'That's when I phoned him. At first he clammed up and wouldn't say a word but, rather than threatening to go down there and beat him up, as you seemed to think, I told him the truth.

'When he was convinced I meant it he gave me your address and wished me luck.'

'What truth?'

'That I loved you.'

As she stood absolutely still he leaned forward and rested his forehead against hers.

'I mean it, Charlotte. I love you and I want to marry you...'

So much joy flooded through her that it was impossible to contain it all. Her eyes filled with tears which overflowed as Daniel went on, 'I was hoping against hope that you felt the same?'

When, struck dumb, she continued to stand there, tears running down her cheeks, drawing back, he said with sudden doubt, 'Or have I made a terrible mistake?'

She found her voice and whispered, 'No, you haven't made a mistake.'

'Then why are you crying?'

'I'm just so happy.'

When Charlotte opened her eyes the next morning the bedside clock showed eleven-thirty.

She was lying snuggled close to Daniel, her head on his

chest. Beneath her cheek she could feel the strong, steady beat of his heart and the calm evenness of his breathing.

Moving carefully, she glanced up at his face. He was still asleep, long lashes curling on his hard cheeks, a dark stubble adorning his jaw.

My love, she thought. Then, even more wonderful, *and I'm his.*

He had told her so over and over again as he had kissed her tears away. Then, settling her on the couch, he had producing a small box.

'Your Christmas present… And just in time,' he'd added as the clock began to chime twelve.

'But I've nothing to give you.'

He kissed her. 'Don't worry, my heart's darling, I'll think of something.'

In the box was the most exquisite ring she had ever seen—a flawless emerald flanked by diamonds.

When he slid it on to her finger she found it was a perfect fit and looked wonderful on her slim but capable hand.

'I intended to give it to you three days ago. When I woke and found you'd gone I was devastated…

'Woman—' his voice was husky '—if you only knew what you've put me through.'

'I'm sorry. I'll try and make up for it.'

'I'm pleased to hear it.'

Their lovemaking had been… But even words like *rapturous, ecstatic*, weren't enough. Such a flood of feeling was indescribable.

She had discovered love swiftly, shatteringly, and, because of the circumstances, cruelly. Now everything had changed. So much happiness would have been unimaginable just the previous day.

Lifting a languid hand she traced his mouth, the roughness of his jawline, the cleft in his chin… 'Wake up, sleepy head… There's only an hour before lunch.'

She gave a squeak of surprise as, without warning, he rolled, pinning her beneath him.

Eyes gleaming silver between half-closed lids, he drawled, 'Plenty of time to teach you who's boss around here, Ms Charlotte.'

Bending his head, he kissed her until she was breathless.

When he drew back a little, fluttering her eyelashes at him she simpered, 'Oh, but I do love masterful men.'

'If you're trying to win me over you'll have to rephrase that.'

'Sorry. I mean I do love a masterful man.'

'That's better. Now, what's it to be, a cup of coffee or—?'

'A nice cup of coffee would be wonderful.'

'Serves me right for asking,' he said ruefully and kissed her again before getting out of bed.

He was impressive enough dressed, but naked he was magnificent, with broad shoulders and the long, supple build of a swimmer.

While he found his robe and pulled it on she watched him with her heart in her eyes.

She was still lying contentedly, recalling all the pleasure the night had brought, when he returned with two mugs of coffee and climbed in again beside her.

They sipped their coffee in companionable silence and both mugs were empty before she asked the kind of question that maybe all lovers ask. 'Daniel, how long have you loved me?'

He drew her close. 'When does a passionate desire become love?'

'When it takes you over, possesses you, I suppose.'

'In that case I've loved you since the moment I set eyes on you. I called it desire then, but it had already taken me over, possessed me. I could think of nothing else but you.

'When Telford told me that Tim was your stepbrother I

wanted to come straight to you then and bring everything into the open.'

'Why didn't you?'

'I thought it might be too soon, that you might need a little more time. I was afraid you'd refuse to listen to me…

'So I went back home and tried to think what to do. That's when I came up with the plan for exchanging staff. I was hoping very much that you would apply for the transfer.'

'What would you have done if I hadn't?'

'I would have thought of something else. I'd waited all my life for you, and I had no intention of letting you go…

'Will you be happy living in New York?'

'Ecstatic, if you're there.'

'I'll be there.'

'Speaking of New York, weren't you planning to go back today?'

'Do you want to?'

She shook her head. 'Not now. Though I love the thought of going back to The Lilies, I'd like to stay here for a few more days. If we have enough supplies?'

'Mrs Munroe's brought in sufficient for a month. Which reminds me, I'm hungry… Maybe happiness gives one an appetite.'

It certainly *suited* him, she thought. He looked younger and more handsome than ever, his smile ready, his eyes glowing.

'How about you?' he queried. 'Are you hungry?'

'Starving.'

'Tell you what, as we still have to bring the car back, let's walk over to Marchais and have a celebratory lunch there.' With a little squeeze he added, 'I can't wait to tell someone *our* good news.'

When they got outside they found it was snowing lightly, dusting everything with a coating like sifted icing sugar.

As they set off along a secluded path through the trees Charlotte asked, 'Does all this land belong to the lodge?'

'Yes, it's private ground as far as the perimeter fence which runs along the far side of the wood. Tomorrow, while the snow's good, we could try a couple of the ski trails…'

'Sounds wonderful,' she said happily.

'Alternatively, we could stay in bed,' he suggested wickedly.

'Sounds even more wonderful.'

'That's my girl!'

They were walking between banks of snow-covered bracken when, straying a little off track, she found herself almost thigh deep.

'Daniel,' she asked dreamily, 'have you ever made love in a snowdrift?'

Alerted by her tone, he answered guardedly, 'No.'

Smiling at him, she began to unzip her anorak.

The cushioned ground was as soft as a goosefeather bed, and snowflakes drifted down mixed with fine particles of frost from the taller fronds of bracken.

The combination of heat and cold, fire and ice, was sublime, and she found herself thinking that if angels ever made love this was what it must be like.

As she floated back down to earth she opened her eyes and, looking up at Daniel, saw that his neat ears were red and there were tiny ice crystals on his long lashes.

Guiltily, she asked, 'Do you think I'm mad?'

Brushing a few flakes of snow from her face, he kissed her cold lips and said, 'Undoubtedly. But, in my opinion, you've never lived until you've made love to a mad woman.'

Introducing a brand-new miniseries

For **Love** OR **MONEY**

This is romance on the red carpet...

For Love or Money is the ultimate reading experience
for the reader who has a taste for tales of wealth and
celebrity and the accompanying gossip and scandal!

**Look out for the special covers
on these upcoming titles:**

Coming in September:

EXPOSED: THE SHEIKH'S MISTRESS
by Sharon Kendrick #2488

As the respected ruler of a desert kingdom, Sheikh Hashim
Al Aswad must marry a suitable bride of impeccable virtue.
He previously left Sienna Baker when her past was exposed—
he saw the photos to prove it! But what is the truth behind
Sienna's scandal? And with passion between them this hot
will he be able to walk away...?

Coming soon:

HIS ONE-NIGHT MISTRESS
by Sandra Marton #2494

SALE OR RETURN BRIDE
by Sarah Morgan #2500

HARLEQUIN®
Presents~

Seduction and Passion Guaranteed!

www.eHarlequin.com

HPTSM